PROJECT NYX

THE LONG RUN: BOOK TWO

LEAH R CUTTER

KNOTTED ROAD PRESS

Project Nyx
The Long Run: Book Two
Copyright © 2022 Leah Cutter
All rights reserved
Published by Knotted Road Press
www.KnottedRoadPress.com

Cover Art:
Illustration 113789435 © Tiziano Cremonini | Dreamstime.com

ISBN: 978-1-64470-309-0

Cover and interior design copyright © 2022 Knotted Road Press
http://www.KnottedRoadPress.com

Reviews
It's true. Reviews help me sell more books. If you've enjoyed this story, please consider leaving a review of it on your favorite site.

Come someplace new…
Are you a traveler? Do you enjoy exploring strange new worlds, new cultures, new people?

Journey into the various lands envisioned by Leah Cutter.

Sign up for my newsletter and I'll start you on your travels with a free copy of my book, *The Island Sampler.*

http://www.LeahCutter.com/newsletter/

ALSO BY LEAH R CUTTER

Science Fiction

The Long Run

Project Nemesis

Project Nyx

Project Tisiphone

Project Persephone

War of the Allied Worlds

The Labors of Darius Linard

Huli Intergalactic: Science/Space Fantasy

Origins

The Strawberry Girl

Urban/Contemporary Fantasy Series

The Cassie Stories

Poisoned Pearls

Tainted Waters

Spoiled Harvest

Bloodied Ice

The Witch's Progress

Circle of Air

Circle of Fire

Circle of Water
Circle of Earth

Seattle Trolls
The Changeling Troll
The Princess Troll
The Fairy-Bridge Troll
The Troll-Demon War
The Troll-Human War
The Troll-Troll War

The Shadow Wars Trilogy
The Raven and the Dancing Tiger
The Guardian Hound
War Among the Crocodiles

The Clockwork Fairy Kingdom
The Clockwork Fairy Kingdom
The Maker, the Teacher, and the Monster
The Dwarven Wars

The Chronicles of Franklin
Franklin Versus The Popcorn Thief
Franklin Versus The Soul Thief
Franklin Versus The Child Thief

Epic Fantasy Series

Houses of the Dead

INTRODUCTION

I've always referred to the first book in this series as *Leverage* meets *Star Trek*. Though, by the later books, I was referring to the series as *Leverage* versus The Evil *Star Trek* Federation.

Leverage holds a very special place in my heart. I mean, who doesn't love good competence porn? (And if you haven't seen the TV show *Leverage*, it's like the movie *Ocean's Eleven*, only done in a weekly format. Capers with a revenge theme.)

The writers on *Leverage* were awesome. John Rogers has a special place in my heart, to be honest. I was able to ask him once about whether or not the writers had ever heard of Lester Dent.

His response? The essay by Lester, which details how to write modern fiction, was printed out and hanging on the wall of the writing room. (Here's a link: http://www.paper-dragon.com/1939/dent.html)

I started this series with the concept of a five-man band. I did a lot of world building, figuring out what the equivalent of a phone would be, what the transportation mechanism was, as well as the aliens.

I also started by using Damon Suede's *Activate* method,

basically, coming up with a verb for each character, then using those as the inspiration for all their actions and interactions.

This has been a blast to write. My first readers have each had a favorite character, however, they'd all had a *different* favorite.

This is a good problem to have.

I hope that you also enjoy these books, this lighter take on crime and the future.

Enjoy!

Leah R Cutter
July 2022
Ravensdale, WA

CHAPTER 1

JUDIT

Judit Kovács, Human captain and pilot of the starship *Eleanor,* still wasn't sure if she wanted to vomit or not.

She sat alone in her quarters. The screen to the side of her desk showed a live feed of the secondary engineering room. Basil, her engineer, worked feverishly, inching as fast as one of the Oligochuno could, going from one busted cooling pipe to the next, trying to stop the leaks. Other members of the crew did what they could to help.

In the center of the secondary engineering room, on the small dais there, stood Judit's quandary.

Judit had believed Eleanor, *the person*, when she'd said that she, Gawain, and Abban were members of the race known as the Chonchu. The smart systems that made up the ship *Eleanor* were, well, too smart for merely AI. Judit had suspected that there was something different about them.

She'd just been dreaming too small. Hadn't allowed herself to be paranoid enough.

Hadn't even *considered* that the three personalities that *Eleanor* displayed might, in fact, be *people*.

Judit shuddered again at the implications.

The three Chonchu stood on the dais in the secondary engineering room. Parts of their biological forms had been fully encased there, in what looked like three amber spars. Brain, spinal cord, and a few other essential organs, transferred to a new form and put into service.

Judit felt her stomach knot itself in new and interesting ways. She was still considering vomiting.

It didn't matter to her that the three were Chonchu, an alien race that she didn't really know. Evidently they were originally an aquatic race, and operated with a connected, hive mind. Without at least three Chonchu beings present, they lost the ability for independent movement, and fell into something of a fugue state. Which was why there were three of them.

She didn't care that they'd volunteered for the gig, considered it an honor.

All right, so it was pretty cool that the three of them might never die if this experiment worked out.

Still.

They were people. Enslaved on *her* ship. Eleanor had sworn they'd volunteered. More than once. There'd been so many volunteers for the program that the queens of the Chonchu had held a lottery. They could have stepped down at any point in the process.

Nothing that Eleanor had told Judit made her feel any better. Honestly, at this point, Judit wasn't certain what would.

She was still too much in shock over Eleanor's revelation. Still processing what exactly it meant to have not just smart systems, but actual living consciousnesses as part of the ship. What other experiments that Arthur, the crazy Yu'udir who'd started this project, had been indulging in.

Besides enslaving members of an alien race.

Judit sighed and pushed herself away from her console. She wasn't going to solve any of her issues tonight.

Tomorrow would be time enough to solve this issue. Along with all the other problems they might face.

One day at a time.

Or as her mother had always jokingly said, *Egyszerre egy kecske:* one goat at a time.

JUDIT SAT ALONE in the space that had been configured for her office. It was located between the two primary helms on the spaceship *Eleanor*, in what she considered the bow of the ship.

It wasn't a large space. Just enough for a desk, two guest chairs on the far side of it, her work chair behind the desk, and a larger, more cushioned chair pushed against the far wall.

The plain, gray desk stretched across the front, which conveniently blocked easy access into the rest of the room. It was bolted to the wall on one side, with a narrow opening on the other. Judit could slide through it with centimeters to spare on both her front and her back. Though she was in her forties, and maybe, *possibly*, had a few extra pounds on her, she wasn't overweight or "squishy" by a long shot. She just had womanly curves. Besides, most of her weight was muscle. She regularly worked out in the small gym on the ship, doing her pushups, bench presses, and dead-weight lifts.

Currently, Judit sat in the comfortable chair at the back of her office. Arthur, the crazy Yu'udir who'd built the ship, had offered her a full range of fabrics, materials, and designs for it. He was, or had been, into that sort of thing, all of the conference rooms on the now destroyed space station

Camelot designed by a set designer, each of them with a different theme.

Judit had only taken advantage of a few of the modern conveniences that a purpose-built chair offered. She hadn't wanted a monument to comfort. She just wanted a nice chair she could sit in and look out the porthole at the stars. The chair was covered in a stain-proof fabric—probably a good idea given how much coffee she drank—and it was a lovely peach color. The fit against her legs and butt was perfect. And the cushions were made from a supportive gel that was similar to the pilot's couch in the main helm, that exact right mix of soft and firm.

She'd had the walls of her office painted different colors: two were a deep forest green, while the other two were the softest, lightest blue. Somehow, the contrast helped keep Judit balanced. She hadn't really personalized her office beyond the small sticker of a red tulip—the Hungarian national flower—stuck to the wall just above where the edge of the desk was attached. The little statue of the gray *puli* dog that she kept for good luck had been destroyed, back on *Camelot.*

The ship hummed quietly to itself as Basil, the Oligochuno and chief nerd on her crew, continued to enact repairs. They sat in an uninhabited corner of space while they assessed their position.

It had been four days since they'd entered the Wolpol system, heading for home, only to find that the space station *Camelot* had been destroyed. It was only because *Eleanor* had broken down a few days beforehand that they'd escaped being blown to pieces themselves.

That also meant they were going to be running low on supplies soon. They hadn't stocked up for a long run.

The replicator—basically, a 3-D food printer in the kitchen galley—was going to have to be restocked with chemicals. The ship was pretty self-contained in terms of water, but some still evaporated out of the system. That, too, would need replenishing.

There were several space stations that both Judit and her second-in-command, the Yu'udir Saxon, knew of that wouldn't look too closely at their credentials.

Getting there wasn't the problem.

Having enough credits to pay for everything, as well as being able to leave again, was much more of an issue.

Judit had closed the door to her office while she'd been contemplating their next move. However, she'd left the green light on outside, meaning that if anyone knocked, she'd answer. She rarely flicked on the red light and isolated herself in here.

No, if she was in a really foul mood, she'd take it out on the weights and fighting dummies in the gym.

Judit flicked through star systems on her screen. All of them were merely a short run from where one of the hyperspace gates dumped you into a system, that is, merely lasting hours to days.

Judit wouldn't consider a long run, not in general, and particularly not now. A long run would take months to get from a hyperspace gate to the nearest planet.

Even the thought of a long run made Judit homicidal. Xenocidal. Whatever.

The loud rap on her office door brought Judit back to the present. "Come!" she called.

It didn't surprise her that Basil inched zir way into the office.

The uneducated might say that the Oligochuno resembled an earthworm. Zie stood about one hundred and forty centimeters tall, though when laying down Basil could stretch out almost two meters. Zie had a skinny, pinkish-gray segmented body and tended to have awkward bulges along the sides where Basil stored zir tools, in specially grown, internal pockets.

Instead of eyes, Basil had an orange sensing ring that took up the upper third of zir head. Though others complained about never being able to know exactly what an Oligochuno was looking at, Judit didn't mind. She just assumed that zie was looking at everything, in all directions, at all times.

They'd be great in a bar fight, though Judit had never managed to make one of those happen at the same time she'd been buddies with an Oligochuno.

The year was young, though.

Today, Basil had grown three sets of arms along the sides of zir torso. The top pair seemed to be the strongest set, the biceps muscular, though there weren't really shoulders. The other two sets were more delicate, each with just a finger or two, all of which were probably specialized. One might be a sensing tool, while another might be a type of screwdriver.

Judit heaved herself out of her comfortable chair and went to sit at the desk. The Oligochuno didn't really sit: instead, they flattened out the back of their tail and just leaned back, resting.

"What's up?" Judit asked, taking back on the role of "captain" for her crew.

"I've done all the repairs that I can, with the supplies on hand," Basil said. Zie sighed.

Judit had been learning much more about the body language of the Oligochuno since working with this crew. She thought that Basil was tired. The color of zir body was more gray than pink and zir skin looked dry. The orange of zir sensing array had also faded. Like other Oligochuno who'd spent time in the company of Humans and Yu'udir, Basil had learned how to smile with the thin line that was a mouth of sorts.

Right now, that line was definitely turned down along the edges.

When Basil didn't continue, Judit prompted zim, "But? I hear a big ol' *but* coming in at the end of that sentence."

Basil sighed again. "But I need additional chemicals in order to replicate the cooling systems that were initially installed."

"How rare are these chemicals?" Judit asked. "Are we talking a large, multi-planet star system with access to huge chemical factories? Or will most any space station have what we need?"

Basil thought for a moment, before tilting zir head from one side to the other. For races that didn't have shoulders, it was the equivalent of a Human or Yu'udir shrug. "Medium to large," zie said. "A smaller station might not have them."

"So, somewhat specialized," Judit said. "Any idea how expensive this is going to be?"

"No," Basil said. Zie sounded surprised. "I'll have to do some research."

"Good," Judit said. She paused, then decided, what the hell. "Is continuing doing the right thing?"

"I'm not sure what you mean," Basil said slowly.

"There are three *people* trapped in that secondary engineering system," Judit said. She'd been having this conversation with herself and Saxon mostly. It was time for the rest of the crew to weigh in with their opinions.

"Not trapped," Basil said firmly. "They chose their fate."

Now, it was Judit's turn to sigh. "I know. Eleanor told us that. How, among the Chonchu, the opportunity to work beyond the Hive mind is considered a great honor. Do they still feel that way, now that they've lived here for awhile? Will they still feel that way ten years from now? Fifteen? One hundred?"

Basil brought one of zir smaller specialized arms up. It

had two fingers initially, rapidly joined by a third that sprouted out beside the others.

"First, I have no idea how I'll feel one hundred years from now. And they are alien, as alien to me as I am to you. *We* cannot answer that," Basil said, folding one finger down. "Second, as far as I can tell, yes, they are very happy with their decision. They've both gained more independence while remaining a single hive than anyone had predicted. They are, all three of them, highly satisfied."

Basil folded down a second finger, so only one remained. "The question that you didn't ask was how they feel about working with us. They have no station to return to. No Merlin to report to. Masala really was an engineering genius who could fix any problem they might have."

Judit blinked. She kind of had asked that in the second question, but it hadn't been as focused. "All right," she said after a moment. "How do they feel about us?"

"They like us," Basil said, folding the fingers of zir hand together and drawing the arm back. "They're a little pissed off at Masala right now, though. Did you know that the overheating and system failures were built in?"

Judit tilted her head from side to side. "Doesn't surprise me. It's an additional leash that Arthur had on the ships, so that one couldn't just break free."

"I've been fixing the problems permanently as I've encountered them," Basil said. "But it's going to take time. And more materials."

Judit felt the decision she'd been putting off weighing down on her. Though the crew ran mostly as a democracy, with every member getting a vote, in the end, she was the one they all looked to for guidance.

"Will *Eleanor* be all right without your care for the next twelve hours?" she said, sitting up straighter.

"She will," Basil said. "She's stable right now."

"Then go get twelve hours of sleep," Judit directed Basil. She held up a hand before zie could complain. "After you've rested, we'll hold a meeting and vote on which system to go to."

Basil nodded slowly. "All right," zie said. Zie abruptly pivoted, inching out of Judit's office, closing the door behind zim.

Leaving Judit with the second half of the puzzle she needed to figure out.

Chemicals cost credits. As did general supplies. While they'd all been paid well in Arthur's program, none of them had the credits to support a spaceship that was going to need a lot of repairs in the short run.

Luckily, *Eleanor* had been built as a cargo ship.

What was to be her first haul?

CHAPTER 2

MENEFRY

It was time for Menefry to meet with the rest of the crew. Time for them to decide their fate.

He'd spent longer than usual with his morning prayers to the Goddess Nesnefera—may her eight limbs forever weave the pattern of days—settling himself more firmly on the path he'd chosen.

Now, he just had to convince the others that his way was the right way, as if the Goddess herself had blessed it.

The woodlands conference room was not Menefry's favorite. Nor was it his least favorite. No, that horror went to the winter room, the walls covered in a holographic image of ice and cold blue skies, forever bleak and chilly. Menefry's favorite conference room was the desert room, where the walls appeared to be sand dunes dotted with scrub and stones. However, Menefry had also claimed that room as his office, spending most of his time in there and not at the secondary helm at the bow of the ship. Therefore, no one tended to call meetings in it anymore.

Which left the woodlands conference room. The walls were covered in holographic trees and the air always held the faint scent of pine. While it was cooler than Menefry liked, having grown up on Calacktik, the desert home world of the Khanvassa, at least it was tolerable. He enjoyed the quiet chirping of small insects in the background, and his eyesight was good enough, even in the twilight of the room.

He could tell that the room left Judit on edge. She would glance around occasionally, as if seeking predators hiding among the trees. The Bantel, Kim, seemed to enjoy the room, and had joked once about wishing the trees were real so she could climb them.

Saxon, the Yu'udir, didn't appear to have much of an opinion one way or another, along with Basil.

Menefry timed his arrival in the conference room so that he would be the last. Everyone else was already seated on chairs appropriate for their physicality, except for Basil, who stood, leaning back on zir tail.

"Good," Judit said, nodding his way as he settled himself down on his kneeling chair. The large hard shell he wore didn't allow him to sit like the other beings, who all had unprotected torsos. He folded the middle set of his arms over his tunic, which was covered in a light brown vest.

Arwenphtat had always said he looked good in brown. But he couldn't allow himself to think of her now, just to pray that the Goddess in her infinite wisdom might see to reunite them someday.

"Eleanor, can you join us?" Judit said, calling the primary being of the ship into the room as well.

A hologram that Menefry had never seen before sprang up on the solid wood table that filled the center of the room. The image looked like a large spur of amber growing out of the flat surface, maybe thirty centimeters tall and about half that wide. It took Menefry a moment to recognize that it was the current physical manifestation of Eleanor, her body encased in a solid organic substance that fed and maintained her.

While Judit and some of the others might have been having difficulty with Eleanor's chosen path, Menefry did not. The Hive mind that the queens generated seemed to be a clear descendant of the Goddess. And what was Eleanor's form but a cocoon, a type of chrysalis? The Khanvassa weren't born with their shells. They transformed. The current state of the three beings who formed the core of the ship were also in the middle of a transformation.

What they would turn into, he didn't know. But he firmly believed that they were all walking the paths laid down by the Goddess with her many arms.

"Thank you for inviting me," Eleanor said. "I will speak for all of us."

Judit frowned. "Should I have invited the others?"

"No, that won't be necessary, not for this meeting. But for others, yes, it might be."

Menefry clicked his mandibles together softly in approval. Judit was rough around the edges. For a Human, she wasn't a bad fighter. Nowhere near his level, but she would hold her own with untrained fighters. Plus, inside that lumpy shell was a solid interior, a heart beating in tune with the song of the Goddess.

"We've come to a decision point," Judit said. "Basil has made all the repairs zie could, given the supplies on hand. Zie needs additional chemicals and materials to continue repairs."

Menefry nodded along with the others. Judit had been good at communicating the state of the ship to them regularly.

"So we're faced with several decisions to make this morning, several paths, as it were," Judit said, with a nod in his direction. "Do we want to continue working as a crew together? The answer to this question cannot be assumed, and must be settled first, before we get into anything else."

"I'll start," Kim said cheerily. The Bantel's top was a particularly strident shade of sickly green. Had she thought that perhaps she could blend into the trees in that? Her scaly skin was a non-complementary shade of lime green, and her large eyes bulged pink and red. "I think we should stick together, for a while. At least until we figure out if anyone is after us. Then we may need to each go our own ways."

"I concur with Kim's assessment," Basil said. "Together, until we can get more intel." Zie sounded tired, though zir coloring was better than it had been the day before, more of a pinkish gray than a grayish pink. Today, zie had no arms protruding from the sides of zir tube-like, segmented body. At the same time, the sides of zir torso were particularly lumpy, as if carrying half of zir toolset with zim.

Judit turned to Saxon, who nodded slowly. The Yu'udir had on a dark brown vest today, which went well with his white fur. His blue eyes peered out of a black face, taking in the entire room before he spoke. "I concur, that our most expedient choice for now is to stick together. I also fervently hope that we will be able to continue working as a crew long after we determine our fate."

"Menefry?" Judit said, looking at him.

Menefry clicked his mandibles together once, for luck. "Yes, I believe we should work together. Like Saxon, I hope that our paths continue together for the long run, not just a short one."

"Eleanor?" Judit said. "Do you accept us as your crew for the time being? Or do you want us to stop at the nearest station and start interviewing a replacement crew?"

Eleanor laughed at that. It was the most delightful sound. Menefry had often thought that the Goddess must frequently send ripples of laughter throughout the universe to lighten their hearts and brighten all the worlds. Lately, he'd been of the opinion that the laughter of the Goddess was akin to the sound of the ship.

"We'd like for you to continue as our crew, now and always," Eleanor said. "As long as you're willing to lead us, we'll follow."

"Aye," Saxon said solemnly.

Judit nodded. "I had thought that would be everyone's position, but I wanted to have it spoken out loud, rather than assumed. I will draw up some very simple, very basic contracts for our continued partnership."

Menefry couldn't help but smile at that. Of course, the Human wanted a contract, one that the Yu'udir would probably vet. Their word was never good enough, not for this sort of serious venture.

While Menefry understood the importance of a contract, he personally didn't need one. His word was his honor. He would do what he said. For better or for worse.

"As I said at the beginning of this meeting, Basil has done as much as zie can with what is on hand. But our supplies are going to start running low, soon. Plus, Basil needs specialized chemicals to continue zir repairs. It takes a lot of credits to keep a ship going. I can't afford to support *Eleanor* on my own, out of the wages I have saved up from Arthur. None of us can, not even if we pool together our credits. So we are going to need to pick up cargo and do a run. Sooner rather than later."

Again, everyone around the table nodded at this. No one was surprised.

"Eleanor, could you please go over your transport capacity?" Judit said.

"Gladly," Eleanor said. As she went through the numbers, everyone nodded.

It wasn't a lot of space, Menefry knew. Most cargo ships had many times that amount of cargo space.

However, the space was heated and pressurized, so they could carry more delicate cargo. In addition, they could guarantee quicker runs than a standard carrier.

Menefry had been counting on that, actually.

"So we're going to need to stop in a system where we can pick up a specialized job, while at the same time, get chemicals for Basil," Judit concluded.

"Plus, we need to be able to contact our sources, to see if there's a bounty on our heads. Or if there's anyone looking for *Eleanor*," Saxon pointed out.

"This means I'm open to suggestions for which station or system we should visit first," Judit said. "Eleanor, I'm going to ask you first."

"Thank you," Eleanor said. "But I don't have a good idea of where we should go. I have a large amount of statistics at my fin tips, so I can tell you about almost any system we go to. However, I know almost nothing about all of them."

It gladdened Menefry's heart that Eleanor was starting to use more of her people's vernacular when she talked with the crew. He'd heard others describe the Chonchu as a fish-like race, at least in their appearance, even though they were a land-based species now. They'd originally been aquatic, and it was still present in their vocabulary.

"Menefry?" Judit said, evidentially going in reverse order to the first time they'd spoken.

Menefry leaned forward, resting his weight-bearing arms on the cool wood of the table, folding his fingers together. "I think we should go to the Djeda system," he said. "I can guarantee us cargo to transport. It's a big enough system that we would be able to get everything we need. I can probably get credit extended to us, at least enough to cover our initial expenses. And I would be able to get in contact with my network, to see if there's a price on our heads."

A hologram sprang up beside Eleanor's amber spur. It showed the Djeda system: three settled planets, a handful of space stations around each, and active traffic throughout the area.

Menefry found it interesting that Eleanor not only showed the Cartel's hypergates, but the less predicted gates as well, the ones that only someone such as Abban could access.

Could they access one of them without alerting everyone in the system that there was a new, different exit? He wasn't sure.

"Calacktik is the main world, right?" Saxon said, leaning forward. "We've been there once?" he said, looking to Judit.

"Twice," she said.

"Would they welcome you back?" Kim asked. "What?" the Bantel said, leaning back when everyone glared at her. "It's a legit question."

"It is," Judit said. She raised her hand before Saxon could growl. Again. "We didn't get into too much trouble while we were there. But what about you, Menefry?"

"There was some unpleasantness before I left," Menefry said smoothly. "However, enough time has passed that there shouldn't be any further recriminations."

Really, the Goddess said that you should forgive those who had repented and done the work of overcoming their short fallings. And he had.

Hopefully Kemere would see that. Arwenphtat as well.

Kim also had a suggestion, some Bantel world. He knew that Judit would never go for it. She had a deep, abiding mistrust of the Bantel.

He wasn't about to tell her that it had not been Brett, the Bantel on her last ship, who had turned against her. He held that information like a jewel lifted up by the Goddess's right foreleg. At some point, it would be the right time to tell the pilot.

Just not now.

As no one else had a strong preference for where they should go, Menefry knew that they would select the Djeda system. Fall into the Goddess's intended role for them all.

He was just a shepherd to guide them along the way.

CHAPTER 3

KIM

Gosh, it made her so *mad* that Judit wouldn't trust her! Kim was doing everything she could to be a team player, to get along with the others. She'd even been sure to change the fine scales of her skin to extra bright colors, to help cheer everyone up.

She was surprised that Menefry hadn't told them about the extra surveillance footage she'd been acquiring of all of them.

But as he hadn't, there was *no reason* for the rest of the crew to not trust her!

She wouldn't have just taken *Eleanor* without them. She knew she couldn't. The ship had to agree to let itself be taken.

That was, until Kim finished putting back in several of the "leashes" that controlled the ship. Arthur and his Merlin, Masala, had originally installed them. Basil had been diligently removing them. Kim had been just as diligent in replacing them. She needed those in place so that Kim could steal *Eleanor* for herself.

But now wasn't the time. They really did have to work

together for a while, until they figured out which was the easy tunnel out of their predicament.

She did have to admit that she liked the name that Saxon had given their team for the time being: Project Nyx. It referred to an old Earth myth about a goddess of darkness.

And that was who they needed to emulate, at least for the time being. Hiding out in the dark while they gathered information.

Kim paced back and forth through her rooms. She hadn't bothered really personalizing them. It was a big enough space, larger than some of the safe houses she'd built for herself over the years.

There was a front sitting room, where she could entertain at least five other people if she so chose. It held three couches done in butter-soft gray material, along with over a dozen bright, colorful pillows that could be used for building a nest on a couch or on the floor. She kept the walls an off-white, the perfect accompaniment for whatever outfit she chose to wear that day.

Just past that stood a small kitchenette, with a food-reheater and a fridge. She would admit that she was very partial to the strawberry sorbet that Eleanor had introduced her to. A plain black cupboard held the few dishes she regularly used. Opposite that stood the cleaner and refresher. *Eleanor* wasn't stocked with enough water for a proper bath or shower. That would just have to wait until they found a planet somewhere that had a ton of water.

It sure wouldn't be where they were currently going.

Kim had purposefully kept her bedroom looking as plain as the rest of her rooms. A soft, round bed in one corner she could nest in, a wardrobe made out of the same black material as the cupboard at the foot of the bed. A chair sat, forlorn, beside it. Over the bed, a large display hung.

The only thing one might find odd was that the longest

wall in her bedroom was completely clear. Nothing hung on it. The wardrobe had originally been attached to it, but she'd moved it the other wall. It felt as though one half of the room was crowded with furniture, while the other half was empty.

Kim kept it that way on purpose.

A special holographic generator was built into the empty wall. Kim regularly used it to train her reflexes when it came to changing the color of the fine scales that covered her body. The display over the bed could be used to show vids, or even static artwork.

It also worked as a mirror, enabling Kim to see just how closely she matched the background she was working with.

None of the others knew just how well Kim could hide in a location. Not only did she have better control of her scales than most, she also had special equipment to help keep her hidden. She had a suit that would reflect the ambient temperature of whatever room she was in, so that she couldn't be detected with a heat monitor. She had a generator buried in her backpack, used to project images onto the suit, which helped her hide in a variety of pre-planned spaces. Plus other advantages that a modern-day thief needed.

Now, while Kim hadn't been able to talk the others into going back to the Gamor system where she would have access to all *her* contacts, that didn't mean that she was going to sit by and let Menefry run the entire show.

No. She was certain she could find people in the Djeda system. And her contacts were going to be of more use than anyone else's. That was for certain.

All the rest of the crew were mostly honest people who'd had a snag in their career. None of them were a dedicated—professional!—criminal, like her.

Kim took a deep breath in through her snout and out through her tiny mouth. She wasn't getting ready to steal the ship from the others. Not really. She'd make sure that they were all set up in whatever system they chose.

Then she and *Eleanor* could go off and have all sorts of adventures. Like those buddy vids of the two best friends, one of whom was a giant, lovable but dumb Yu'udir, and the other, a plucky and smart Bantel.

It would be so awesome!

In the meantime, Kim could practice her blending in skills more. She called up the holograph of the desert conference room, with the sand and scrub. She could practically feel the heat coming off the baking rocks, smell the musty dirt. She stripped out of her really cute green outfit, then stood beside the wall and held out her hand.

While it was possible for Kim to change in a few microseconds, she always started slowly. Better to get it perfect while deliberately changing so that when she sped up the transformation, everything was right.

The small scales across the back of her hand took on a sand color. Sand, like snow, was surprisingly difficult to blend into. There was such a minute variety of colors in every centimeter. It took skill and patience to get it right.

Once she could no longer see her hand against the wall, she let the transformation proceed, up her arm to her elbow. She stopped for a while, making sure it was just right even as she rotated her arm around before continuing.

After a few more minutes, no one would be able to see her in a desert landscape. She set the pattern of her skin to shift minutely as she moved, so that the edges of her body were more difficult to detect. She also raised her internal body temperature. The monitor told her that she was close to the limits of what she could do biologically.

She knew Bantel who'd been bio-enhanced, so that they had much better control of the temperature of their skin.

Maybe someday she'd want to do that.

For now, she was just going to practice for the desert places they were going to. She kind of hoped they'd get into trouble at some point, just so she could prove to the others that she was trustworthy.

That was, until she stole the ship.

CHAPTER 4

SAXON

Saxon sat alone in his chambers, reading, as Judit called it, lugubrious, gory poetry.

He couldn't help it. He was still in mourning for Arthur, for *Camelot*, for Project Nemesis. That bright and golden future had been snatched away from them all.

He knew who was responsible for it. They all did. The Cartel was the only player who understood just what a threat *Camelot* had represented, the hope that it gave to all, not just the Yu'udir but the other races as well.

The front room of his suite didn't hold a lot from his past life. That had mostly been destroyed on *Camelot*. He still had a few small mementos, such as the tiny spear he kept for luck and his favorite flat cap.

Two large, comfortable armchairs took up much of the front room. They were both made of a soft, plush-like material, an off-white that hid whatever fur he may shed. Although he knew he should keep at least one other chair in there, in case someone smaller than him came to visit, he'd never bothered ordering one. So both chairs were fit to his size. Judit complained that she felt like a child whenever she sat in one.

Maybe after they made their first run he could buy another.

Saxon didn't know what tribe Arthur had claimed as his heritage. Saxon's family swore that their ancestors had come from one of the more northern tribes, where it was warm for only half of the year, and the other half was encased in ice and snow.

Mind you, most of the Yu'udir claimed to have come from such tough stock regardless of their actual lineage.

The world he'd grown up on had been a little more temperate, though it did have a good deal of snow. His older brother and sister still lived there. Saxon hadn't returned in a decade or more, though he regularly sent and received messages from his family. Even with his supposed death, Basil had given him a way to stay in touch with them.

He knew that they'd keep his secret safe, and would never reveal that their brother still lived. It hurt that he couldn't talk with his nieces or nephews anymore, but they'd all decided that was for the best. They'd had a memorial service for him.

His brother, the bastard, had even sent him pictures of it, which had arrived in the last set of message packets, transmitted regularly system-wide.

In ancient times, the Yu'udir had built death towers. They were raised off the ground far enough so that four-legged predators couldn't access them. But there was no roof. Instead, the bodies of the fallen would be placed there, exposed to the harsh climate. Predatory birds could still tear the bodies apart, and frequently would.

Some of the older death towers had a thick layer of bones across the top, the finery placed beside the bodies long since disintegrated.

The legends said that all those souls would be summoned to the hall of the dead, overseen by Aredhros, the god of the dead. Those who had done their penance or lived especially good lives would be welcomed into the hall, thawing out their bones by the great fires. The others stayed outside in the cold until they'd paid their dues.

Great heroes, kings, and queens were all made to be servants in the hall of the dead. While humble warriors and farmers, widows and children, were seated at the grand table and fed a banquet.

It wasn't enough for a single person to behave with civility and graciousness, no matter their station. Everyone attending the feast that evening had to play their part. Nobility had to be truly humble, and the lowly former servants couldn't grow too proud.

If they all worked together, everyone in the hall for that evening was allowed to depart through the back door of the hall, not the front. Out there, they would find golden fields and easy prey, a paradise for the rest of their days.

When, inevitably, people misbehaved, they were sent back out the front door, back into the freezing cold to await their turn again.

Saxon didn't believe in any of those sorts of fairytales, neither the gods of the dead nor of the living.

Still, he understood at a deeper level what the symbol of *Camelot* had represented, painted gold like the paradise of those ancient tales.

So he sat in his rooms and read old poetry, filled with brave heroes, dashing maidens, weeping widows and avenging sons.

And contemplated his deep-seated need for revenge before his own bones were exposed to the cold of space.

CHAPTER 5

CLAYTON

CLAYTON WAS STILL GETTING reports of the damage that had been done in the Wolpol system, to the space station *Camelot*.

Every single one of them made him smile.

Even the reports from the science nerds who were trying to determine what such a large, physical explosion had done to the stability of the hyperspace tunnels. Seemed some ships had had difficulty traversing from the tunnel leading to the Wolpol system immediately after the space station had been destroyed.

Some were advising that they should shut down that system for good.

More's the pity.

Clayton read through the reports in his own office. It was official Universal Trading Cartel business, as far as he was concerned. One of their competitors had just been blown to bits.

Really, he was going to have to stop chortling at that.

His office was located in Armadillo system. He'd tried every so often to get it renamed to Texas, to reflect the glorious state that his ancestors had come from, but Armadillo was close enough.

He lived on the space station *Dallas*, the largest of the three in this system. There were four habitable planets close by, along with another couple of dozen at the ends of various long runs.

His office reflected the past. The holograms on the walls generally showed scrub and painted hills, maybe a dozen or so longhorn cattle grazing in the distance. He had an actual set of horns hung on the wall behind him.

Too bad he couldn't place the head of a Yu'udir there beside it.

Instead of books and scholarly tomes that would only impress the eggheads, Clayton had spurs decorating the walls of his office, along with a coiled bullwhip and a few antique rifles that officially weren't in working order. Clayton might have bent the rules there a little. He had an old saddle in the corner, and made sure that the staff always kept it freshly polished, so the office always carried the faint masculine scent of leather.

The chairs in front of his desk were done in bloodred leather with brass tacks around the edges. His own chair was the only nod to modern times, as he really needed the support after sitting for too long. A thick carpet of dark green and wood paneling on the walls that weren't sporting the hologram completed the look.

This was a serious place, where serious business got done.

And Clayton was engaged in serious business. That was, when he wasn't cackling with glee over the reports about *Camelot*.

Really, Sachiko was worth her weight in gold. No one had had any warning before the station had just exploded. He still wasn't sure how she'd done it, and though he wanted to know, he couldn't.

Plausible deniability and all that.

He could just imagine the look of shock on Arthur's face as his entire world imploded. Exploded. As his dreams were all exposed to the cold harsh vacuum of space.

There was really only one detail that remained.

Universal had tried more than once to infiltrate *Camelot* and Arthur's project. However, no one had been able to worm their way in. It wasn't that Arthur's security team was that good. Just that Universal hadn't had the chance to find the right lever.

The one thing they could keep track of were the ships that Arthur and *Camelot* had registered. Not all those ships made it off the dock, or were space ready.

Universal kept track of all of those registrations and compared them to the record kept of all ships that left the Wolpol system.

Not all gates kept such records. Occasionally, those records would be deliberately lost by a system due to bribes. Other times, those records were only kept for a short amount of time, say, a few months.

If Clayton had had his way, all of those records would be kept for ten years or more. How could Universal truly track all traffic through the gates if they only had a few months' worth? How could they plan ahead or see trends?

He'd managed to get a few directors to listen to him, but not enough. Maybe now, though, since their attention wouldn't be divided by *Camelot*…

The one detail that was still open was the ship registered as *Eleanor*. More than once one of Arthur's ships had never made it back to port. Eventually, insurance claims were filed.

Eleanor, like the other ships in Arthur's experimental fleet, made frequent short runs. Those ships would go out and return in one to two days.

Except that *Eleanor*, as far as Clayton's sources had been able to discover, had never returned to the Wolpol system.

Universal didn't keep track of ships returning to a system, just leaving. But for *Camelot*, they made more of an effort to track all traffic. Unofficially, of course.

Had *Eleanor* been disabled somewhere along the way? Fallen out of hyperspace and imploded?

Clayton could just write the ship off. However, he wasn't prepared to do so. Not yet.

Instead, he continued to keep track of all ships entering any of the bigger hyperspace tunnels. The program he'd had set up would alert him if she returned from the dead at some point. At least for the next five years.

Then maybe he'd kill that particular search routine. Maybe not.

Universal hadn't gotten to where it was by being sloppy, or short-sighted.

So maybe after ten years, he'd check that box and announce that *Camelot* and all those experimental ships who'd sprung from her unholy womb were truly, officially dead.

CHAPTER 6

BASIL

Basil didn't like lying to the rest of the crew.

Technically, zie wasn't lying. Given enough time, zie really would be able to fix all of *Eleanor*'s systems, get them to work as well as they had been, the last time they'd departed *Camelot*.

That was, if enough time wasn't limited by the heat death of the universe.

Zie had made great strides. *Eleanor* was mostly functional. However, she was going to be prone to breakdowns until they'd replaced most, if not all, of her systems, both in the secondary engineering room and quite possibly with the secondary engine system as well.

Though Basil mourned the death of *Camelot* with the rest of the crew, zie still wasn't sure if zie was happy about Masala being dead.

In the most ancient tales of the Oligochuno, if even a segment of a great hero remained, zie could regenerate, regrowing from that small piece. It had to be a complete segment, all the way around the torso, not just a slice from it, as the idiot Chunaseko discovered trying to save zir mate in the old myths.

Basil knew those were just fairy tales. Still, zie would have liked to be able to resurrect Masala, just so that zie could strangle zim to death. Slowly. Painfully. Maybe secrete a paralyzing substance from zir skin, so that Masala couldn't struggle as Basil crushed zim with zir tail.

It was an unforgivable sin, as far as Basil was concerned, to cripple a ship like *Eleanor* as she had been. Forcing her to suffer overwhelming heat. The Chonchu were originally an amphibious species. They needed the cold as much as the Yu'udir.

Deliberately sabotaging the ship's cooling system was sadistic.

However, it was also completely effective. Overheating was the fastest way to bring the secondary engines, those operated by Eleanor, Gawain, and Abban, to a standstill.

Basil had accepted the help of the others for some of the larger repairs that zie had enacted, such as replacing many of the cooling ducts in the secondary engineering room. But a lot of the finer, more delicate repairs zie had had to do on zir own.

At least now if there was ever any overheating, Eleanor, Gawain, as well as Abban would notice it. Those sensors had been among the first that Basil had replaced. And then enhanced, as well as built in redundancies.

Basil stood in the secondary engineering room, surveying zir space, noting the repairs that had been done, those that still were necessary. It wasn't a large room, maybe three meters on a side. It was set off from the primary engineering room by a specialized wall that only Eleanor controlled. The wall wasn't aware, not like a person. However, it had a biological base and responded to her emotionally (psychically?).

That was something else that Basil didn't understand. It was possible that zie would never know enough to be fully understand.

Eleanor, Gawain, and Abban were three separate beings. Each of them had started off as a regular member of the Chonchu species.

The Chonchu had a hive mind. They needed at least three of them in close contact for them to operate. An individual member of that race didn't have the awareness necessary to interact with others. They had great queens who ordered their society and controlled the individuals of the species.

How exactly did the queen communicate with all of her subjects? How did the hive mind work? Were they psychic? Or was there a more rational, reasonable explanation?

Eleanor couldn't explain it. And Basil didn't have either the time or the resources to do the experiments zie longed to do, to figure out this grand mystery.

No, zie had to stay focused on the job at hand, mainly, get them to the next port and continue enacting repairs.

The original walls of the secondary engineering room had been lined with green tubes, filled with a viscous liquid that kept the room cool. Now, the walls had a combination of the green tubes and the replacement parts that Basil had cobbled together. The crew had agreed to close off one of the transport cubes used for cargo so that Basil could salvage parts from it.

While some of the tubes were the original green material, the rest were a shiny silver. Patches of silver covered the green on the tubes that were still standing.

Eventually, all of the green tubes would need to be replaced. Along with the viscous cooling substance that Masala had evidently invented. Basil had never seen anything like it before. Like everything else, it had a biological base and wasn't just a soup of chemicals. It reacted instinctively, oozing into the areas that were warmest without any software intervention or monitoring.

The tubes continued from the second engineering room, down through the room containing the primary engines, to the secondary engines that were attached to the very bottom of the ship. None of the crew had EVA equipment so they hadn't been able to go outside the ship to investigate those engines.

At least Eleanor had cameras that could show Basil the secondary engines. They looked like a set of black square boxes, all different sizes, that had been attached together. The array was large, several meters wide as well as long, spread across the entire bottom of the ship between the two main engines.

Getting an EVA suit was Basil's first priority once they reached a larger system.

Honestly, though, all that was secondary to Basil's main concern, which was the interface between the three Chonchu and the secondary engines.

Eleanor, Gawain, and Abban stood in the center of the second engineering room, appearing as three amber spars. They ranged in height between one hundred fifty-five to one hundred seventy centimeters, while the base of each was roughly sixty centimeters across. The surface of each was very lumpy, like a molten heap of wax that had been allowed to cool.

Basil had looked using all of zir senses, but zie really couldn't see the being encased by the amber. There were small white lights—maybe a dozen for each—that blinked off and on inside of each spar, but those each appeared to have their own heartbeat.

The three of them stood on a round dais that was raised about thirty centimeters from the floor. They formed a lopsided triangle, with Eleanor, the tallest, on the left toward the back, Abban, the shortest of them, beside her on the right, and Gawain in the center, though closer to Abban than to Eleanor. All the connections between them and the ship ran from the foot of the spars through the dais.

Basil had removed as much of the dais as zie could so zie could get into the guts of the system.

And that was where he faced his biggest conundrum.

All of the wires that led from Eleanor, Gawain, and Abban were biologically based. There might or might not be a copper wire running through the center of what looked like a mass of muscle meat.

Repairing those would take more skill than Basil felt zie currently possessed. Zie had ended up using the food printer in the kitchen to replace wires that had been roasted by the heat.

It was a patch job, at best. The wires zie created weren't as good as the originals. Gawain and Abban complained about the sluggish response they now received from the engines, when before it had been instantaneous.

Those wires needed not just a bio-enhanced specialist, but their own unique printer.

Given time, perhaps Basil could fix all the wires. Maybe even improve them. For now, they'd have to limp along with what they had.

Eventually, zie was going to get the captain to purchase a second food printer that zie could modify and use in engineering.

"Scale for your thoughts?" Eleanor asked as Basil still sat back on zir tail, looking around.

"I feel as if I'm failing you," Basil admitted. "I've fixed everything as well as I could, but—"

"Shhh," Eleanor said. "You've done a marvelous job. We understand the massive task that you've been given. Software is your forte. Not bio-wear." She paused, then added, "We wish we could be of more help. Tell you exactly what has been done to us, how the process works."

"I know," Basil said. Zie gave them a smile, though zie wasn't certain if they could detect that or not. "I just hope the others understand that we're all doing the best we can."

"They will," Eleanor assured zim. "Though Judit still has problems with accepting our form."

"She has a good spine," Basil said, using the vernacular of zir species. "She will do the right thing and go along with the consensus of the group. She would have you choose your own destiny, even if that means flinging yourselves into the heart of a sun."

"Masala removed that choice from us," Eleanor said.

"I know," Basil said. "And I promise you, I will return that functionality to you as soon as I figure out how."

Masala had had more than one technical genius working with zim on Project Nemesis. Basil honestly hadn't had the time to rewrite all the code that went along with all the wiring. Getting the systems operational, as well as making sure the cooling systems worked, had been zir top priority.

Removing all the leashes that Arthur and Masala had set was distinctly second.

"We will be in a larger system soon," Basil continued.

"One hour, nine minutes," Gawain noted.

"I'll get all the chemicals I can, to replace your existing cooling system," Basil promised. That was one of the problems with the viscous liquid that Masala had been using: It needed to be replenished. Or fed. Or something. After too much time, it turned brown and started to stink of rotten algae.

"And a suit for yourself?" Eleanor inquired.

"If I can find one," Basil said. All of the species required their own suits. As they were heading into a Khanvassa section, zie didn't know if zie could find one that would fit zim. Not without paying several sections of tail.

"Good," Eleanor said. She paused, and gave that expressive sigh. "Will we be safe at this station?"

"As safe as we can be," Basil said. "Menefry says he has a cousin who runs one of the smaller space stations. We'll dock there, away from the main hub."

While a smaller station might mean more scrutiny because there wouldn't be as much traffic in or out, Menefry swore that since his cousin owed him a favor, it might also be a lot safer.

It all depended on whether or not Menefry was lying, and if this cousin would repay her debt.

"Someday, you will need to update all the locking mechanisms on the ship," Eleanor said. "Change them so that we control them, so that only those whose DNA we know can have access."

Basil nodded. He hadn't bothered bringing up Eleanor's idea to the rest of the crew yet.

Too many species had nightmares and horror tropes for what happened when you allowed a ship, a machine, to control everything.

But *Eleanor* wasn't a machine. Not at the heart of her.

Just an set of aliens who no one had ever really met or understood.

CHAPTER 7
MENEFRY

Menefry breathed a sigh of relief, clicking his mandibles together, once, twice, when he heard Nirdjsy's voice on the other end of the comm line, welcoming them to the space station *Atwak*.

The space station filled the screen Menefry had called up in front of him. Instead of working in the desert conference room, he'd joined Kim in the secondary helm.

One thing that all spaceships had in common, across all the species, was redundancy. Two helms, so in case something went wrong with the one, they could still work the ship from the second. Two engine tubes, so that if one stopped working, you could still limp home on the other. Twice as many escape pods as there were crew members. Two 3-D printers so that if the food printer died, you could swap out the chemicals on the one in engineering and keep making food.

And so on.

The secondary helm looked similar to the primary helm that Judit and Saxon worked from: gray-green walls, golden chairs for the two occupants, black rubber-like floor covering that gave you good traction, and huge windows across the front so you could bathe in the glory of the Goddess and her universe. The space was still cramped, between the two chairs, the two occupants, the two consoles and the rest of the controls.

Menefry's kneeling chair didn't take up that much space. However, the Khanvassa were a much larger species than the Bantel, not just taller but so much wider, mostly due to the heavy shell. So his "side" of the helm extended well into Kim's side.

The Bantel appeared to take that in stride, never complaining about the tight fit. She wore a truly remarkable shade of pink that day, blazing with all the strength of a setting sun.

Atwak was an old station. It wasn't shiny like *Camelot* had been, but done in various shades of black. It also wasn't symmetric in the least. The core of the space station lay at the heart of the mess ahead. Then modules had been added, building out the station a bit at a time. It looked like a child's building blocks that had been shaken up together in a box, then dumped out and glued together however the pieces had fallen.

Menefry had been to *Atwak* before, but it had been several years. He distinctly remembered one of the main food courts. Someone with a sense of whimsy had decorated it to look like an ancient bazaar, complete with clay walls and canvas tarps over the walkways.

Arthur would have liked it.

Nirdjsy said that she would meet the ship when it arrived. There were no huge landing bays on the station, where Judit could just drive *Eleanor* in and park in the interior. Instead, there were personal airlocks for smaller ships along with huge cargo airlocks for transporting containers.

The cargo doors were on the side of the ship, so Judit had to align the middle of *Eleanor* with the station. At least four other ships were also attached to *Atwak* nearby, offset both above and below them, like a set of stairs made out of ships.

Kim grinned at Menefry when Judit announced that they were successfully attached to the station. "This is so great! I've never been to a Khanvassa station before."

Menefry tilted his head from side to side. "It will be like most of the other stations you've been to," he said. He wasn't lying, not quite. In many ways it was just a plain, ordinary station.

The main difference would be the appropriate statues and altars to the Goddess one found everywhere.

Menefry waited until Kim had gotten up and left the helm before he stood. The ceiling was tall enough that he didn't brush his horns against it, though when he raised his upper, load bearing arms above his head, his fingers did touch before he could fully stretch his arms out.

Still, Menefry spent a few moments loosening up, twisting his head from side to side, bending and straightening his torso, as well as stretching out his other set of hands. He had a plethora of knives and other weapons hidden under his shell, as well as under the golden sand-colored vest and reddish pants he wore.

He didn't expect trouble. But the Goddess favored those who were prepared, just in case.

For a short moment, Menefry folded all of his hands together and bowed his head, asking one last time for the ever-weaving eight legs of the Goddess to set his path clear.

Then he lifted his head and marched out of the secondary helm, down to the cargo bay that held his fate.

CHAPTER 8

JUDIT

Judit always forgot how *huge* the cargo holds on *Eleanor* really were. If the ship sort of looked like a woman wearing a skirt with her arms raised when viewed from above, from the side she more resembled a pregnant lady. While much of the rest of the ship was all on a single level (which made it more useable for a mixed-race crew) the cargo holds dropped down significantly. There were stairs, a lift, as well as ramps that led from the top level down into the bowels of the holds.

Judit waited with the rest of the crew while Menefry took the stairs down to join them. He jogged up and down the stairs on a regular basis, as part of his continual training. Judit had tried it once and decided that she didn't need to add that particular level of hell to her life.

If you didn't include Kim in her searing pink outfit that was guaranteed to start your eyes bleeding once you stared at it too long, the rest of the crew looked vaguely professional. Saxon was in a pretty blue vest that made his eyes stand out and his white fur look brighter. He also had on a matching blue flat cap. Basil didn't wear any clothing. Zie just had zir usual grayish-pink tubular torso that had extra bulges today, holding more equipment.

Judit had known to wear something lighter. The *Atwak* station was likely to be warmer than she liked. So she had on a short-sleeved shirt, the color of reddish sand. Her pants were short, cropped just below the knee, and she wore thick black sandals.

Menefry had told them not to expect trouble, but to go into the station armed, just in case. Judit had her favorite hand cannon attached to her hip. It was stronger than the beamers that people usually carried, and shot a large massive gout of pure energy instead of a skinny beam. It was like getting hit in the chest with a cannon ball, except that the ball was made of fire and burned. It had about the same range as a regular beamer with three times the hitting power.

Judit was aware that it looked ungainly attached to her waist and hanging down almost to her knee. It was awkward to use, particularly if you weren't trained, didn't practice shooting with it regularly, and didn't have both the muscles as well as the weight to handle it.

Those aspects just made the gun more special to Judit. And it made opponents underestimate her. She didn't look like someone who could handle such a big gun, and no one understood just how diligently she trained. Possibly not even Saxon.

Saxon carried something similar strapped to his waist. It looked less cumbersome on him; then again, he stood a good head and shoulders taller than Judit.

The hand cannon wasn't his favorite gun. He actually preferred a little beamer. It looked like a round gray disk and fit perfectly into the palm of his black hand. The button on the top triggered a long, deadly beam. Its range was about two meters farther than the hand cannons, which made it the perfect accompaniment.

Judit would bet that the palm beamer was tucked away in a pocket someplace. Along with a few other, possible less-than-legal weapons.

It was difficult to see how Menefry felt when he reached the bottom of the stairs and came striding toward them. His big brown eyes didn't show any fear, and his hands fell naturally at his waist.

His only tell was how his mandibles appeared to twitch every now and again, as if he were constantly wanting to click them together, for luck if for nothing else.

"We'll be fine," Judit told Menefry as they stood on their side of the airlock, waiting for the other side to open. The cargo door would easily fit two smaller ships to pass through side by side, perhaps eight meters wide and twice that tall. It was designed that way, so that small skids tugging containers could enter and leave at the same time, speeding up the process. The door would slide to the side, inside the skin of the ship, once the airlock opened on the far side. Right now, it stood like a huge segmented barrier, the lights along the edges of it all flashing red.

Finally, an audible click came from the other side of the door, and the lights turned green. Slowly, the door started to open.

Three of the Khanvassa stood in the opening. Without seeing the back of their shells to check for color, Judit would bet that the one in the middle was female, while the other two were males, just based on their size. All the Khanvassa stood over two meters tall, but the one in the center was slightly smaller and Judit would say had more delicate features.

Plus, the station master was female, and the two standing behind her looked like armed goons, each carrying their own hand cannons.

Menefry said something in a melodious language. Judit

assumed it was both a greeting as well as a prayer. He'd given the crew more than one benediction in his native tongue so she recognized at least what it was, if not the words. She was always surprised that a creature as large and as awkward looking as the Khanvassa had such a beautiful spoken language.

The one in the center of the trio facing them—Nirdjsy, Judit would bet—gave a similar greeting.

It was impossible to tell if one of the Khanvassa was smiling. Their mouths and mandibles just didn't work that way. Sometimes, that sort of emotion was carried in their bottom set of hands, the fingers waggling or soft in a way that told the viewer they were joking.

Nirdjsy's hands formed into fists as she said, "You have a lot of nerve showing your shell here."

"I have done the work of repentance," Menefry replied smoothly, his own lower hands staying neutral. "I deserve a chance to prove myself."

"I'm not the one you should be proving yourself to," Nirdjsy said, her hands still clenched.

"Each journey starts with a single step," Menefry said in retaliation. "Why not start with you, then work my way up to bigger things? Bigger problems? Bigger apologies?"

"Not hearing any apologies," Nirdjsy pointed out.

"Cousin! You wound me," Menefry said. "When have I wronged you?"

Judit opened her mouth then shut it again. She was going to have to talk to Menefry about his diplomatic skills.

Suddenly, all of Nirdjsy's fingers started wiggling. "Cousin! How I have missed you," she said. She took two steps forward and lowered her head.

Menefry also stepped forward and they briefly touched their horns together. It took Judit a moment to remember what the gesture stood for. It was their equivalent of a Human or Yu'udir hug.

The cousins straightened up, though they still held hands with their middle set. "You are looking well," Nirdjsy said, looking Menefry up and down, before she took another step back. With a wave of her hand, the two guards turned and disappeared into the airlock. "Now, introduce me to your latest crew."

Menefry introduced them, using the fake names they'd all chosen, along with their position—pilot, navigator, communications, and engineer.

"Which leaves you as the security?" Nirdjsy said, looking to Judit to confirm. At Judit's nod, Nirdjsy said, "Smart choice."

That made Menefry stand up even taller. If a Khanvassa could smile, he'd be beaming.

"You are welcome to my space station. I run a loose ship, as there's much more profit that way, so you are all expected to be adults and take care of yourselves," she warned.

"Yes, of course," Saxon said, sounding more like a stuffy British college professor than ever before. "We will be delighted to do business with you."

Nirdjsy bowed her head, then linked arms with her cousin and started pulling him toward the station. "So tell me everything, all the gossip you've heard," she said easily.

Judit wasn't worried about Menefry. He wouldn't talk too much about *Eleanor*. None of them would. They'd used a different registration for her when they'd identified themselves to the station: *CC-211*, the good ship *Mourning Dove*.

Hopefully the registration would stand up to scrutiny, though she wasn't too worried. Anything Arthur had done would probably have been top notch.

"Want to go explore?" Judit asked Saxon as they also proceeded into the station.

"My dear, I thought you'd never ask," he said.

Judit couldn't help but grin. Sure, the ship needed repairs and the crew needed credits. She was going to have to work her ass off to make sure both of those things happened.

But that didn't mean that she couldn't have a little fun on the side as well.

CHAPTER 9

KIM

STATUES! There were statues *EVERYWHERE*!

That was Kim's first impression of *Atwak* station.

They'd walked from one of *Eleanor*'s huge cargo holds, across the airlock, and straight into a similar cargo hold on the station. It had the same sort of funky, dusty smell that you got from storage containers, same rubberized floor, same huge area for stacking goods, similar high shiny lights that made it difficult to hide or blend into the shadows.

But on the far wall was this *huge* mural of the Goddess Nesnefera, her eight legs held open as if she were welcoming everyone into her embrace.

It was kinda creepy.

Outside the door to the cargo hold sat a smaller golden statue, just past the door in a corner. This one had four arms up and four down, like she was dancing or something. The air changed too, and Kim smelled the sweet incense that the Khanvassa favored, which was more piney than flowery. (She learned later that it was a type of tree resin, which was totally awesome.)

Another statue stood outside the door of what looked

like a customs office. And another was tucked into a notch just above a hallway. And yet more. Almost every corner had its own statue, all different colors, all different poses.

Some of the statues showed the Goddess as more of a Khanvassa, though she had a smaller shell. Others made her look more like a spider, with eight black legs and a rainbow-colored torso.

Kim knew she shouldn't steal any of them, as much as she might be tempted. Where would she sell it? Even the cute ones were kind of creepy, with all those arms that looked like they might come alive just grab you, and she didn't want something like that in her rooms on the ship. Would make her nest uncomfortable.

Instead, Kim focused on finding others of her kind.

Not other Bantels. No.

Other thieves.

She'd asked Nirdjsy which sections of the space station that they should avoid, in order to stay out of trouble. Then she headed to those directly to scout out the area. *Atwak* didn't have a lot of tourism, so it was really easy to fall off the beaten path, to end up in sections where only Khanvassa lived and worked.

Kim couldn't hide her appearance. She was a Bantel, and everyone would know that by looking (down) on her. She was only a meter and a half tall, while most of the Khanvassa were over two. It would make it easier to hide when she needed to, as she'd be out of direct line of sight for the most part.

It was gonna be so much fun blending into the walls at some point! She'd have to wear a more "work-like" outfit to make that happen, though.

She buzzed through the area quickly, surprised at how close a "normal" neighborhood butted up to the bad areas. How much spillover was there? Or did everyone just know that on this side of the street, you behaved, and on that side, you didn't?

After her tour and a few discreet inquiries, she headed back to the ship to relax and prepare for the following day. Instead of practicing more of her camouflaging techniques, she spent the evening curled up in her nest watching spectacularly silly Khanvassa soap operas. She couldn't help but giggle at all the contortions the actors went through in order to be "bad" but still not step so far over the line that a priest or priestess might be called.

The next morning, Kim toned down the color of her skin, making it sandy-brown. Instead of the really cute pink outfit she'd worn the first day, she'd changed into a much darker brown shirt and shorts. She changed the color of her eyes to a lovely golden brown, in honor of the Goddess.

Then she slipped out of *Eleanor* unseen and unnoticed. She knew that Judit and the others would have had some choice comments about her subdued appearance.

This was what she wore for *work*. Since she didn't do this kind of work on the ship, what was the point in dressing down? No, much better that they didn't realize she could be this discreet.

Kim had made some inquires the day before about the types of ships that didn't look too closely at the cargo they carried.

Instead of learning of one or two names, she'd quickly acquired dozens.

Seemed that *Atwak* kind of specialized in smuggling. Who would have thought such a thing? Kim certainly hadn't!

Not all of the Khanvassa were as pious as Menefry, so most of what got smuggled into *Atwak* were narcotics that worked on the Khanvassa but not any of the other races. The equivalent of really good mushrooms for the Bantel, the kind that made you sleepy and dreamy and see lots of amazing colors.

What got smuggled out were weapons and security systems. Menefry being a security guy made more sense now.

For breakfast that morning, Kim wound her way through narrow passages and past pedestrian bazaars to a small neighborhood café just a few blocks from the area she'd been warned about. Someone had recommended that maybe, perhaps, she might find what she was looking for there, in terms of a ship that wouldn't pay too close attention to what she was shipping off planet.

The café sat on a corner, close to the large market. It had a nice, neighborhood feeling, the kind of place that would start making your order as soon as you walked in the door once you became a regular. A long counter stretched across the back of the café, while the rest of the space was taken up with round tables and multiple kneeling chairs, the sort that Menefry used.

The counter itself was too tall to be comfortable. Kim didn't have to stand on her toes to see over it, but she would have had to in order to rest her elbows on it comfortably. Behind the counter, hanging on the wall, was a list of all the drinks the café made. The back counter held the equivalent of three industrial-sized blenders and a couple of juicers.

Good. No coffee maker. She shuddered. Humans were so weird in their addiction!

A small statue of the Goddess stood on a shelf above the equipment. The statue itself was black, though it was swathed in gold gauze, with a cute red peaked hat. Large gold coins—probably made of base metal and then painted gold —were scattered at the Goddess's many feet.

The café, though everything was oversized, still felt intimate to Kim. The walls were painted a dusky brown, a soothing color. Some sort of white stone covered the floor, shiny and easy to clean. The smell of fresh grass and fruit filled the space. It had windows on two sides, with another counter there so people could stand and look outside, in addition to the four round tables in the center of the floor, each with at least half a dozen of those kneeling chairs that Menefry liked around them.

After Kim ordered her drink, she went to stand at the counter looking out the front window. None of the chairs would have fit her, and standing made the counter (almost) a comfortable height.

While most of the menu contained things she couldn't digest—who knew there were so many different types of grass?—it also had a huge list of the various Khanvassa fruit smoothies.

Including something that Kim had only tried for the first time the day before—bubble drinks. The "bubbles" were a chewy gelatin-like substance formed into small balls. They were gummy and delicious. She'd never seen them before on any station.

She'd export them in a heartbeat. Might make a fortune too. Maybe she'd just have to steal the recipe, or the machine that made them.

Though Kim had really wanted a donut that morning, the fruit drink she'd gotten instead was quite lovely. It was made fresh, from a yellowish fruit that tasted similar to a Human banana, both sweet and starchy. The bubbles were perfect—chewy and slightly tangy.

The street outside the shop had a constant parade of Khanvassa walking along, going to and from the market. More than one of the older males or females had a group of young children tagging along behind them. They were cute in a way, though they kind of looked like small black slugs with tiny black shells.

It was easy to tell the gender of an adult Khanvassa based

on the color of their shells, just like you could tell a female Bantel from a male by the neck ruff.

It certainly made sense that they'd decorate their statues with all the colors, since their shells came in all those colors as well.

Just as Kim was finishing up her drink (and debating ordering a second) a voice from beside her asked, "Is this place taken?"

Startled, she looked up into the eyes of the Khanvassa standing beside her. Strange. She hadn't heard him approach.

If she had to guess, she'd say that he was older. His brown eyes seemed softer and the edges of his shell not as sharp, as if worn down with age. He only had a single horn intact: the other had been broken off some time ago, the edges of it still jagged.

"It is now!" Kim said with a smile. "Please. Join me."

"I am Wasimy," the Khanvassa said with a bow of his head. While Menefry's shell was an iridescent blue-green, Wasimy's was mostly solid dark blue, with just a hint of red around the edges.

"I'm Fai!" she chirped. "I'm just visiting for now. But I'm keeping my eye out for ships that I can use in the future," she confided. She used the name for the identity that Menefry had created for her. All Bantel used one-syllable names that were gender neutral for their given name. She would only use her family name in the most serious of circumstances. It was difficult to pronounce, and most races couldn't get the chirp right in the middle of it.

"I see," Wasimy said before he drank deeply of the cup in his hands. It was filled with a thick green liquid. Probably some sort of grass juice. Ewwww.

"I might also be looking for work in the future," he said cautiously.

"Really? That's great! What kind?" Kim said. She couldn't help but beam. Maybe this part of her plan would go well!

Then she could get back to the more serious business of figuring out how to steal the ship.

"I ship things, from here to there," Wasimy said. "I'm always looking for more things to ship."

"Wow! What a coincidence! I'm also looking for a ship to send stuff. Well, people, too," she said.

"Really?" the Khanvassa said. He straightened up a bit. "I'm not sure I'm available for that sort of cargo."

"What? Oh, no!" Kim said. "I'm not smuggling people. That's…that's not right." She knew that there were some systems where the people who lived there were little better than indentured servants. She didn't want to get involved with that sort of thing at all.

As a professional criminal, she had standards.

"Naw, it's just my friend's got this band. *Eleanor* of Aquitaine? Have you heard of them?" Kim asked, keeping her tone casual while at the same time, watching Wasimy like one of the predatory birds of the homeworld myths. You know. Those huge ones, said to carry off full-grown Bantel to go feed their chicks on some mountain crag.

Gotcha. That flinch was undeniable.

The name *Eleanor* meant something to him.

"Ah, no, no, I haven't heard of a band by that name," Wasimy said. "Maybe a ship?"

"Really? There's a ship named after Eleanor? That's so cool!" Kim chirped happily.

The older Khanvassa stared hard at Kim for a few moments, but she just beamed at him.

Poor old man had no chance trying to tell if a Bantel was lying or not. They had perfect control over all their reactions. It would take a really huge shock for Kim to break character.

"Anyway," Kim continued after a few moments,

continuing to spin out her lies, confident that her cover was secure. "The band thought they'd really make a killing here, particularly with their songs to the Goddess. You know?"

"Are they Khanvassa?" Wasimy said, clearly curious.

"Nope. Not a one of them," Kim said. "I think that may have been the problem," she added in a lower voice. "They kinda need to get out of town sooner rather than later, if you catch my drift."

"The orthodox don't take kindly to blasphemy by outsiders," Wasimy said dryly.

"But they were totally trying to honor the Goddess!" Kim complained. "Anyway. You got anything they might be able to use? Slip off the station in a quiet, unseen way?"

"I might," Wasimy said after a few moments. "Here, have your friends call me." He slid a card, an *actual business card* across the counter.

"How cool!" Kim took out her i-stick—*not* the golden one from *Camelot*, but her generic one, the one that she'd also toned down that morning, so the color along its sides went from the palest yellow to the darkest brown. She read the information on the card into her i-stick, then handed back the card.

She knew of all sorts of tricks that people played with scanned cards, the micro-pixels that could be imbedded in the thicker fonts, infecting whatever i-stick read it. She wasn't worried about it. The program she used for reading his card had isolated the information, encapsulated it in a safe corner. She wouldn't dig it out until later, after she'd double-checked it for all kinds of snoopy bugs that might be attached.

"I hope to see you again," Wasimy said as he finished his green drink. "May the Goddess follow your path and keep you safe."

"May her divine light always light your path," Kim said, happy that she'd asked Menefry ahead of time the sorts of sayings that would be appropriate for use when talking to people.

"In her name," Wasimy said, bowing his head, then turning and leaving the shop.

Kim stayed, toying with her glass, still debating whether to get a second drink or not.

She didn't know for certain, but she'd lay good money that *Eleanor* was being tracked. If they ever pulled into someplace using the original registration for the ship, they'd be turned in lickity split.

Hopefully, Menefry would have just as much luck determining their own personal safety.

Kim carried her glass, as well as her former companion's, up to the tray that held used dishes, then sauntered outside the café.

Might as well go see if there was a statue she could steal. Or maybe switch a few of them around. Move the one from the nearby corner across the marketplace, and then the one over there back here.

Grinning and full of fun plans, Kim sauntered away.

CHAPTER 10

SAXON

As Saxon had suspected, he was on the verge of miserable the entire time he spent on *Atwak* station.

The food was horrifically bad, all machine-made and not seasoned well at all. The Khanvassa didn't have any appreciation for meat, or really any know-how of cooking. The only good thing was that most of the other people were at least as tall as he was, which meant he wasn't forever banging his head against door lintels and low ceilings. However, he still felt like he was a beacon for every glancing look. His white fur stood out against all the black bodies.

Worst of all was the heat. Yu'udir had originated on an ice world, where for many of the clans, six months of the year the ground was covered in snow.

The Khanvassa home world was a desert planet. Their stations were always kept far too warm for someone like Saxon.

He wore his coolest vest, the one that had the extra cooling unit built into it, to keep his torso from overheating. It appeared to be made out of a light, blue-green tweed fabric. He had a matching flat cap, made out of the same material, with a cooling gel tucked away inside, guaranteed to last for at least twenty hours in this heat.

He'd be lucky if it lasted for two, given his luck that day.

While Basil went in search of specialized chemicals for *Eleanor*'s cooling systems and repairs, zie had sent Saxon and Judit out to look for the other piece of equipment that zie had deemed critical: an EVA suit made for an Oligochuno.

On the one claw, Saxon was surprised that Basil had delegated this task. Surely zie would want to try it on?

On the other claw, the Oligochuno were all of a similar mass. Their height didn't matter, as they could adapt and stretch or shrink as necessary.

Besides, zie hadn't really given the task to Saxon, but to Judit.

Not because she loved shopping. She looked as though she was hanging on by just a thread, about to start shouting Hungarian curses if a suit dealer brought out one more ancient modified suit that was sure to spring an air leak the first time Basil tried it on.

No, perhaps the Oligochuno had understood just how much Judit loved to bargain. It was an artform that she frequently practiced at, usually against woefully unprepared targets.

The Khanvassa also appeared to appreciate what it took to get a good bargain though. If only they could find something suitable! (No pun intended.)

On the station, it appeared that each major intersection of hallways held yet another market or bazaar. Each had its own statue of the Goddess, blessing the place and all the interactions that took place there.

Almost all of them had some sort of suit shop. It had surprised Saxon, not the least because more than one of them, even the tiniest one, had suits that would fit all the races.

Why were there so many people doing EVA walks? He'd come to understand that *Atwak* was a haven for smugglers. Were the suits so that people, and possibly goods, could be stashed on an exterior bulkhead? That way, if the ship was boarded, no one would be able to find the goods?

He would have to remember to ask Menefry later.

In the meanwhile, they were about to slip into their eighth shop.

He knew that would be a lucky number for the Khanvassa. May the Goddess see to it that they were suitably blessed. (Again, pun not necessarily intended.)

The interior of the shop was stuffy and miserable, like Saxon, as well as reeking with the scent of the incense that was burned everywhere. Gods help the poor fellow who was allergic to the smell. Tall racks holding EVA suits crowded what might be charitably called aisles. Even a Khanvassa walking sideways would still brush against the merchandise. It stank of molding rubber and burnt wire, as if the suits hadn't been cleaned after their latest occupant may or may not have died in it.

The walls were covered in old-fashioned posters for ridiculous looking vids that Saxon had never heard of, such as "Return of the Sand Worm!" which showed a tiny Khanvassa warrior standing with a spear in front of a large, swaying monster armed with a huge array of dagger-like teeth in its gaping mouth.

Were the vids real? Or just made-up titles?

Based on the number of statues in the shop, Saxon assumed that the shop was a little more prosperous than it looked (or smelled). Goddess statues stood in every corner, and there were three standing just behind the counter, instead of usual one. Saxon still didn't understand what every iconic gesture meant.

It was obvious which ones represented happiness,

showing the Goddess dancing. But by the blackest ice, what did the one with two arms on one side out and the rest behind her back mean? Or the one leaping in midair, with three arms up and every other limb spread wide?

Saxon followed Judit further into the store. He had to stick close to her or he would have easily lost her, as everything was at least a half a dozen centimeters over her head. The racks appeared to be ordered by oldest to newest, with the oldest out front and the newer models further in.

Possibly that it was a good way to differentiate your customers, those with money and those without.

The older suits tended to be gray or brown, particularly the suits for the Khanvassa. However, here and there he saw a suit that was half as large, probably meant for a Bantel given the extreme bright color, which this time was orange. There were even a few white suits that he suspected were for a Yu'udir, based on the size.

Judit had finally snagged a long, thin tube that looked as though it would fit an Oligochuno. Beside it, she'd put a suit obviously designed for a Human. The Oligochuno suit had a broad, wide helmet, with the entire top of it made from a see-through material, so the Oligochuno could use zir entire sensing array.

The tube itself was a pinkish-gray, almost the same color as Basil's skin. It had two arms permanently attached toward the top, with extra slots where additional arms could be added as needed.

This suit also had thrusters, both on the back and toward the end of the tail (if one could really distinguish the front from the back). It would help Basil glide through space, like zie was diving underwater.

The Human suit was a burnt orange color with some sort of sports logo on the upper left chest—black background with a ball going through a net and a spaceship's white trail encircling it.

Honestly, it was the first thing to brighten up his day. Saxon really hoped Judit would purchase the suit for herself, just so he could tease her about whatever sport was played with an orange ball that looked like a skull.

The Khanvassa shopkeeper made his way over to where Judit and Saxon stood. He wasn't as tall or as broad as Menefry. He looked less like a warrior and more like a used sled salesman, even without the greasy fur or dirty claws.

Must be something in the eyes, that same furtive look. Saxon kept his growl to himself, though. Mostly.

"The Goddess has certainly blessed your eyes! You've found one of the most amazing bargains I have," the shopkeeper proudly proclaimed as he slid between the racks of suits. The nametag he wore on his bright red-and-white checked vest said Amun. At least the rest of his outfit wasn't trying to outdo a Bantel for color, his pants and soft boots being plain black.

"This thing?" Judit said derisively, lifting up the arm of the Human suit. "I was just wondering if it was good enough for spare parts."

The Khanvassa appeared greatly shocked. "Why would you tear apart what is a perfectly good suit? Just for parts?"

Judit rolled her eyes at the shopkeeper. "The filters all need to be changed," she pointed out. "The powerpack is fried, I can smell the burnt wires from here. And I'd be amazed if it didn't spring a leak the first time I put it through an airlock."

"You wound me!" Amun said dramatically. "These are some of the finest suits I have in the shop. The powerpack is not 'fried' as you so delicately put it. All of the electronics in the suit are new. If the filters aren't up to your standards they can be changed out. And I personally guarantee all the suits that I sell for up to thirty days."

"Thirty days? On what planet?" Judit asked, clearly not impressed.

Saxon kept his smile to himself. It was one of the oldest tricks in the book—proclaiming so many days for a warranty, with the fine print spelling out that those days were counted on a planet such as Kaemely, where each day only lasted one standard hour.

"On the Goddess's homeworld, Calacktik, of course," Amun sputtered.

"Huh," Judit said, obviously not expecting such a straight answer. "And what about this one?" she said. "If I get the Human suit, maybe throw in the Oligochuno one for free?"

"You would break me if you could," Amun said, sounding as if he were near tears. "Turn my wife and five children out into the street."

Saxon would bet that there was no wife, no children. Amun didn't strike him as a family man.

Not unless it was some sort of crime family.

"You would have me offer you my life's savings, just for an essential piece of equipment that should be rightfully given away for free, like escape pods," Judit growled in return.

"Surely we can reach some sort of bargain," Amun said smoothly.

Saxon was proud of the smile that Judit gave the shopkeeper. It was the kind of fierce grin he might see on the face of a successful Yu'udir hunter, though without the blood of her enemy dripping down her chin. Yet.

"Let us bargain, if you think your heart can take it," Judit said.

Saxon didn't like the look of challenge that the Khanvassa suddenly had.

It was going to be a long, long morning.

IT TOOK the better part of an hour for Judit and Amun to reach an agreement. Judit only reached the door of the shop twice, and they never even dropped into racial slurs.

They did question the intelligence of the other, and Saxon thought Judit had scored an extra few points by comparing Amun's intelligence to box of rocks, then adding that the box would be insulted by the comparison. Whereas Amun's claim that Judit was as competent as a celibate priest in a whorehouse didn't work as well.

The pair of them left the shop with both EVA suits, Judit grumbling and muttering Hungarian curses under her breath the entire time. It wasn't until they were a few doors down that Judit finally dropped the act and gave Saxon a huge smile.

"I need a beer," she announced.

"Was it good for you?" Saxon drawled. He was the one carrying both suits, of course. Really, sometimes he just felt like a walking luggage rack, particularly when he went out shopping with Judit.

"I haven't had that much fun in ages," Judit said. She was practically glowing. "And I think I did get us those suits for a bargain."

In the end, she'd paid twenty-five percent less for the Human EVA suit, and only about half for the Oligochuno's. Plus, all new filters had been installed in both suits. She still complained that the power pack on the Human suit would need some work, but that wouldn't take Basil long to fix.

"I'm glad that you managed to be entertained," Saxon said. "Shall we take the suits back to the ship and then come out again?"

There wouldn't be many places that served the sort of alcohol that Judit was looking for. That kind of bar would be in one of the more established areas of the station, and it would be quite expensive as well.

In addition to coffee, the Yu'udir could also tolerate some types of Human beer. A chemical wizard of a brewer had come up with a formula that tasted good to Humans and that the Yu'udir could also enjoy. The rest of the races had their own forms of inebriant—chemically very different from the Human variety, but that worked well for them.

"Yeah, let's go back to the ship, then go get us a well-earned reward," Judit said. She was still practically skipping along as they wound their way through the narrow station hallways back to the cargo bay they'd attached the ship to.

Menefry had already been in contact with a different cousin and had lined up a cargo for them to haul. Saxon and Judit would be meeting with the shipper later that afternoon to work out the final details and sign contracts.

Everything was flowing along like an ice-free river.

Saxon nearly ran into Judit when they turned the last corner and she came to an abrupt halt.

Then he saw why.

Menefry stood with his back to the airlock.

An angry group of at least half a dozen Khanvassa stood in front of him.

Seemed as if Menefry's penitence hadn't been enough.

CHAPTER 11

MENEFRY

Earlier that morning, after seeing Judit and Saxon off on their shopping trip, Menefry decided that it was time to contact Kemere.

They had been best friends, once upon a time. Long before the beautiful Arwenphtat entered the picture.

Of course, they'd both fallen in love with her, so many years ago. For years, the three of them had been a team, with strong friendships on all sides.

But then Arwenphtat had decided to become more than friends. With both males.

Their friendships became fraught with angry words. Eventually, he'd challenged Kemere to an illegal duel.

Kemere had survived, though Menefry had injured him so badly he'd been in hospital for months, with Arwenphtat at his side the entire time.

Their fight and Menefry's incarceration had brought him to the attention of Fran and Arthur. His sentence had been commuted: instead of spending three years in a Khanvassa prison, he would serve out his time working for Arthur and Project Nemesis.

Menefry considered that he was still serving his time, working with the crew of *Eleanor* and protecting them. While he didn't know the full details of Project Nemesis, he was still willing to carry on the work of the piece they did have.

He had spent a lot of hours flat on his back, the most vulnerable position for one of the Khanvassa, praying to the Goddess for guidance. After considerable reflection, as well as both time and distance, Menefry had finally come to realize that the only way to have avoided the duel in the first place would have required him to walk away, right at the start.

And even then, that might not have been enough.

Arwenphtat was as spoiled as she was beautiful. He truly believed that she had been excited by the prospect of two males fighting over her. She had spurred both of them on, while publicly disavowing any knowledge of their conflict.

Menefry and Kemere had been too young, too inexperienced to realize what was happening, too full of hormones and rut to back away or consider their long-standing friendship.

It had been the perfect storm of youth, arrogance, and luck, despite the fact that neither Menefry nor Kemere were all that young—Menefry had just turned thirty, while Kemere was a year younger, and Arwenphtat two years younger still. Menefry had always taken the teasing of his friends for having old wings, as it were. He'd been born with an old soul.

Menefry knew that he couldn't contact Arwenphtat. Not yet. He still had feelings for her. Might always. She'd been his first love. She would always have a place in his heart.

He had truly repented what he'd done to Kemere. They'd been closer than brothers, because they'd met at university and didn't have a history of challenges and fights that they would have had they been young together.

Instead, Kemere helped Menefry with the higher mathematics that seemed to come naturally to him, while Menefry helped Kemere when it came to bullies who thought they could pick on the brainy one.

Menefry should never have challenged Kemere to a duel. At least, not a physical one. Any sort of intelligence contest, Kemere would have won.

But Menefry had wanted to win. Had wanted to have Arwenphtat all to himself. At that point he hadn't been able to think the situation all the way through. Now, he realized that even if he'd won her, she'd never have been faithful to him.

That knowledge, though, stayed on the tips of his wing and never sank in beneath his shell, which was why he still couldn't see Arwenphtat.

So Menefry sent a note that morning to Kemere, begging for his forgiveness and asking that they have an online chat since Menefry was currently in system, at *Atwak* station.

The almost immediate response surprised him. He didn't realize until later that Kemere had been waiting for his note.

Kemere let Menefry know that he, too, was at *Atwak* station, claiming that it must have been the Goddess's plan to bring their paths back together.

When Kemere asked to meet on board the ship, Menefry dissuaded him. It wouldn't be appropriate, and Menefry wasn't willing to have any strangers aboard *Eleanor*. Instead, they agreed to meet at a juice bar nearby.

Only looking back later, did Menefry realize just how much information Kemere was asking about Menefry, where he was, was he alone, and so on.

So Menefry was taken completely by surprise when he stepped out of the airlock on the station to find not just Kemere in the echoing cargo bay, but eight rough Khanvassa awaiting him.

Of course. One for each of the Goddess's ever-weaving limbs. Which left Kemere as the intellect and Menefry as the soft hearted. He could appreciate the symbolism.

"What is this?" Menefry asked, taking a single step backwards. He looked carefully. The group appeared mixed, with two females and the other six males. None of his opponents had weapons. They weren't there to kill him, merely to beat him senseless. Possibly put him into hospital, as he had once done to Kemere.

Menefry could not use weapons on an unarmed group of assailants, even if he was outnumbered. Not and maintain any sense of honor.

Kemere stood to the right, listing to one side. He evidently still walked with a cane, something Menefry hadn't known. The side of his shell where Menefry had bashed him hard enough to break it had been inexpertly repaired. Instead of being solid, it looked like pieces of black shell held together with white scar tissue. One of his horns was still broken off and had a jagged edge to it. All of his hands were functional, but Menefry could see a slight tremor in the bottom set.

"You said you were looking forward to more penitence," Kemere said. "I decided to bring it to you." His mandibles clicked together, almost as if he were nervous.

Or possibly just excited.

"I have repented," Menefry said, turning all his attention to the Khanvassa in front of him. The one on the left was merely a thug. Didn't hold himself with care, didn't have any training. Menefry would drop him first.

The second assailant he would disarm would be the one almost directly in front of him, hiding behind one of the better trained females. This attacker didn't have any training, and was still trying to work up the courage just to join the coming fray.

The other six…they would be more of a problem. He doubted that any of them had trained as he had, but they weren't amateurs, either. The two females were likely to be the toughest. If he could shoot them both first, before the others attacked, he might stand a chance. But he couldn't, and Kemere knew it.

If Menefry remained unarmed, this group wouldn't kill him. Not even accidentally, because of the dishonor that would bring down on their heads. Even thugs understood that.

"You haven't repented enough," Kemere announced. "Not to my satisfaction."

"Then I will not bother asking for your forgiveness," Menefry said, feeling the weight of that statement dropping down on his soul.

He didn't know why he'd thought that perhaps Kemere would ever forgive him for his betrayal.

Some dreams just died hard.

Before the thugs or anyone else could work themselves up to charge in, Menefry attacked first. He struck the thug on his left with a hard elbow to the center of his torso, making him flail as he landed flat on his back. It wouldn't hurt him: the torso of the Khanvassa had a natural armor. The blow was just to knock him over, get him out of the fight.

The rest rushed in before Menefry could drop the second thug.

Menefry's world shrank down to dealing with what was immediately in front of him.

Punch. Pivot. Block. Kick. Flow back. Turn. Elbow strike. Punch.

It was only when the opponent directly in front of Menefry suddenly dropped to the ground that he realized he wasn't fighting alone.

The tall Yu'udir who now appeared where his opponent had been standing was truly welcome.

Now, Menefry heard the Hungarian curses Judit spouted as she sparred with one of the thugs. The Khanvassa had the advantage of height as well as six hands. However, Judit had a longer reach, more upper body strength, and no compunction whatsoever against striking an opponent in his or her most sensitive parts.

She was only Human, and didn't have the same sense of honor that his kind did.

Only three opponents remained standing after Judit dropped hers: the two wily females and Kemere. When Judit turned to go threaten Kemere , the person who had once flowed through Menefry's life like the Goddess and her prayers, Menefry announced, "Enough."

Judit looked at Menefry for a long moment before she nodded and stepped back.

Saxon also took a step back.

The two females looked at Kemere, who jerked his head toward the exit. They nodded and departed, leaving their companions still groaning on the floor. At least the first thug had managed to right himself and was no longer flailing flat on his back.

Kemere spat in Menefry's direction. "I will not challenge you again, as the Goddess continues to favor you. You should leave. Now. *Camelot* is no longer. Your sentence should be re-commuted, back to a prison here. I shall go apply to the proper authorities this afternoon."

He brought his mandibles together one last time, loudly, an ominous click that echoed through the empty bay. With great dignity, he turned and limped away.

Menefry turned to Judit and Saxon. "Thank you," he said. "I had...I had thought..."

"I know," Saxon said, taking Menefry's arm and leading

him back toward the airlock. "Sometimes it's impossible to let go of those dreams."

Menefry nodded. Saxon had taken the loss of *Camelot* the hardest, especially the loss of Arthur, the greatest Yu'udir of all.

"How quickly do we need to leave?" Judit asked as they reached the welcoming doors of *Eleanor*.

"Later today, this evening at the latest," Menefry said. He gave a bitter laugh. "Kemere has forgiven me somewhat, though he'd never admit it."

"How so?" Judit said.

"He told me his plans, that he won't contact the authorities about my sentence until later this afternoon," Menefry said. "He is giving me the chance to escape."

"Couldn't he just be lying about that?" Judit said, seeming puzzled. "To get you to stay?"

"No, he wouldn't lie about such a thing," Menefry said. "He was always the more honorable one."

And that, too, was something that would forever stick in Menefry's mandibles.

He'd behaved dishonorably. And there was no forgiveness for that.

CHAPTER 12

KIM

Kim couldn't help but bounce in her seat. Just a little. Despite the harsh glares that Menefry shot her occasionally.

It couldn't be her outfit. She was looking TOTALLY styling today. Bright green shirt that made her stand out from the softer green walls, pink shorts because duh, pink, and her skin was such a lovely creamy yellow, like a luscious fruit. She looked good enough to eat!

They were sitting in secondary helm, on the first half of the trip away from the Djeda system and the *Atwak* space station.

While the secondary helm was cool—honestly, how neat was it that she and Menefry had their own helm!—it didn't quite fit her. Sure, the couch was comfy enough, and she did like the gold color. But it was far too easy to blend into. It didn't take any effort at all. She assumed that the sage green walls were supposed to be soothing or something stupid like that. If she could, she'd install a dynamic wall system, so she could change the color every day—every hour!—to suit her mood.

"Must you?" Menefry said with a sigh.

Oops. She must have bounced again. But they were going to Gamor! It wasn't her home, where she'd been hatched and raised. It was still a system that she was very familiar with, and had tons of contacts in.

Finally, they could get someplace where she might have a chance of stealing *Eleanor*. Although stealing the ship was never the end game. It was *selling* the ship and acquiring quite a nest egg that was her final goal.

"Sorry," Kim said, trying to modify her behavior. At least a little. Menefry had been extra grumpy since they'd left *Atwak* station.

Having an old friend send a gang of thugs to go beat you up would even dampen her spirits a little. Maybe.

She glanced over at where Menefry was kneeling, in his special chair. It was hard to tell if he'd been hurt during the fight. It wasn't like he had scales that could be busted, like a Bantel. His torso was so black, it hid any bruising he might have had. Kinda cool.

But she could still tell he was hurt. Maybe it was the way he held himself, stiffer than normal, as if his shell had grown thicker. All of his hands still worked properly, and he hadn't broken any fingers. However, now that she was paying attention, she could tell that they, too, were stiff.

"What?" Menefry asked after a few moments.

"How hurt are you?" Kim said.

Menefry looked away from her. "I don't know what you're talking about."

Kim rolled her eyes, even though the expression was totally wasted on Menefry as he wasn't facing her.

"Look. I know he was your best friend. But you beat him up pretty badly over this woman, right? So severely that he's still walking with a cane?"

Menefry nodded miserably.

"You messed up," Kim said.

Menefry turned his head to look at her abruptly.

What, she wasn't supposed to point that out? Too bad.

"Dude. We all mess up. And getting Kemere's forgiveness isn't nearly as important as forgiving yourself," Kim said. "Work on that."

At Menefry's perplexed look, Kim finally said, "What?"

"I didn't expect you to have such depths," Menefry admitted. "But you are correct. I have been working too hard on penitence. Focusing outward. Maybe I need to apply the prayers of forgiveness to myself as well."

"Whatever it takes to get you to stop being such a morose dumbass," Kim said as cheerily as she could.

The way Menefry stared hard at her was kind of creepy. Like he was trying to figure out the fastest way to tear her head from her neck.

But then he totally surprised her and started laughing.

"What?" Kim said. She was just startled. Really. She was *not* offended that she didn't understand the joke.

"No one has called me such a thing for a long while," he said after he finally recovered. "It is a term that friends use. That my friends used to use for me. They always complained that I was too stiff in my shell, that I'd been born with an old soul."

"Yup. You just need to loosen up a bit," Kim said. "Not that we don't like you as you are, though," she added, just so he wouldn't take offense.

"Thank you," Menefry said. He recited a phrase that was long and flowing in his native language, then translated it for her though she was getting better at the Khanvassa primary language, enough to have picked up a few phrases.

May your friends be more numerous than the Goddess's
    ever-weaving arms
and guide you as much as She does on your path.

"That's lovely," Kim said with a huge grin. She stopped herself before she bounced yet again.

Becoming friends with her crewmates was awesome! She hadn't had too many friends during her career. Mostly marks. She'd always planned out all her thefts alone.

She continued to smile even though she felt a momentary pang of doubt. Here she was, surrounded by people who might become her friends, and she was planning a theft. Alone.

It would be much more cool if they could steal stuff together.

Maybe the next time she tried to make a friend, she'd try to make a thief friend.

With that happy thought, she returned to her communications channel, catching up on all the gossip she'd missed while she'd been away.

CHAPTER 13

CLAYTON

Clayton frowned at the report on his screen. There was something off. He just needed to be patient before the pattern would assert itself.

He leaned away from his desk, stretching out his back. He was really going to need to go see Betsy his masseuse soon. She'd get all those kinks out, then make sure he was relaxed afterward. Give him a special massage, all over.

Yes, an afternoon with Betsy would do the trick, after all these hours hunched over a desk.

His ancestors had it easy, riding a horse all day long, roping errant cattle.

In the meanwhile…Clayton stood up from behind the massive desk, walked past the saddle in the corner, and went to stare out the "window." It was just a hologram from Earth's past, showing an area from the heart of Texas, brown and empty. He could imagine the lowing of the longhorn cattle in the distance. The sound of the winds through the harsh scrub. Rough rock covered most of the ground, not soil. This was a hard land, for hard men, not the easy ground that farmers tilled.

It would have been an idyllic life, out on the range. Sure, there might have been some rain and cold. Maybe an angry river to fight against, to save that one calf. He could see himself doing such a thing, being the hero.

Those cowboys never had to deal with what he did. Like the groups of angry Yu'udir who were demanding that the resources of Universal be used to hunt for whoever had taken out *Camelot.*

Stupid Yetis couldn't read between the lines, that being an outlier like Arthur was always going to get himself killed.

It had cost Clayton a lot of money. A tremendous amount, quite frankly. It hadn't decimated his accumulated savings, but he was going to have to be careful for a few years, not invest too heavily in ideas that were only speculative and not a guaranteed return.

He'd build back up his fortunes. And no one would be the wiser about where his money had gone to.

Except that he was already getting dividends on his "investment" in destroying *Camelot.* Invitations to other meetings initiated by serious people with serious problems that needed solving.

Solutions that involved serious money.

At the end of every one of those meetings, Clayton left feeling even better about himself and his decision, regardless of the loss of lives. So many people hated their neighbors, coveted their neighbors' property.

So many wars that he could prevent by destroying the possibility of freedom.

Clayton helped himself to a glass of sparkling water, with the perfect hint of lemon in it. It was exactly what he needed looking out on that hot prairie. He thought back to that dinner party so long ago. The only one who might possibly have put together the conversation about how they would "storm the castle" as it were was Malina. Then again, she was one of the sharpest people he knew.

He had a meeting set up with her later that afternoon, to talk about additional profits that could be made out of the war-racketeering fools.

Beyond the obvious: sell them the guns, the bullets, the plasma packs, and the beamers. Charge them additionally in transportation costs and bribes. Maybe let the other side know what was happening, so they could collect from both sides. Make sure that the fighting stayed isolated, though. It wouldn't do for it to spill off the one planet, or even the single system, and infect other places.

As he drank his sparkling water, Clayton finally put together what might have been bothering him about the report he'd been reviewing.

Every ship that used one of the hypergates was tracked. Most of that data was just noise. There were millions of ships, millions of more trips that were taken every day. Universal had an entire planet dedicated to the computers that kept track of all that data, sorting it, categorizing it, keeping it safe.

Of course, not all the gates produced the same amount of data. Many of the backwater places didn't have the computers possible of storing it all, at least not for a long enough time for it to be meaningful in terms of searching for patterns.

Universal ships made regular trips from such places, or frequently enough, collecting that data and bringing it back to the storage world.

A name on a cargo ship had been flagged for someone to take a look at. The computers could only do so much.

It wasn't *Eleanor*. That would have raised a larger flag. No, it was one of the other ships that had been, at one point, registered to a Yu'udir who Clayton knew had just been a front for Arthur.

What was one of *his* ships doing all the way over in the Djeda system? That didn't make sense, based on the type of ship that it was—small, specialized cargo carrier.

Clayton strode back to his desk, pulling up the report again.

That was what had pinged his radar, stepped across his boundary marker and set off his alerts. So many ships that had been registered to Arthur that had never flown a single day.

That this one was making its first journey *after Camelot* had been destroyed was suspicious.

He had nothing more to go on, other than that. The Djeda system was rife with smuggling, so truly detailed reports were never made.

Now wasn't the time to try to crack down on the Khanvassa homeworld. Everyone was feeling a little twitchy since *Camelot* had been destroyed. Smart leaders were all wondering if they would be next.

There wasn't enough in the report for Clayton to issue some sort of search order for the ship, or to try to get it boarded for an inspection. They hadn't even filed where they were going. Or if they had, that information hadn't been recorded, as was the case for over three fourths of the ships leaving that region.

Clayton drummed his fingers on his desk. He reached too abruptly for his glass of sparking water and ended up spilling it across the surface of his desk.

Damn it all!

He angrily buzzed his secretary to come in and mop it all up.

Then he was going to issue a very quiet order. The next

time that particular ship left a system, he'd like to know about it.

CHAPTER 14

BASIL

Basil finally, *finally* figured out what that damned viscous green material was that Masala had used to cool *Eleanor*'s secondary engines.

Of course, it was an algae. But a complicated one that needed both heat as well as a rest time in order to duplicate itself. If it didn't have both, it died, turning brown with an odor that even Basil found challenging.

While Basil wasn't an organic chemist, zie was an Oligochuno. Zie did have a better intuitive grasp of the chemical nature of most materials than anyone other than a specialized chemist with access to a large laboratory.

The algae had tasted *awful*. Zie still felt as though zie had ghost fragments of it on zir tasting element. (The uninformed might call it a tongue. It was so much more complicated than such a simple organ as that, though. It looked like a long tube that Basil extended from zir mouth, exactly thirty centimeters long but only a few wide. It tended to take on the color of whatever it tasted. It still looked green when Basil checked it in the mirror zie had borrowed to get the pirate's eyepatch right.)

But by taking the algae into zir body, zie had finally been able to break apart the chemical structure.

It had been a decidedly unpleasant experience that zie hoped to never have to replicate.

Fortunately, zie now had all the chemical knowledge necessary to replicate the material.

The question was, did zie really want to?

Zie sat in the main engineering room, outside of secondary engineering, at the primary monitoring system. Three separate screens displayed graphs of all the systems currently running, that Basil had access to. A large control panel was inset into the workspace, filled with levers for even finer control.

To zir left, the 3-D printer chugged merrily along, printing out additional conduit. Judit had vetoed buying a third 3-D printer just for the bio-mechanical parts he needed. At least not until they showed a profit.

The first cargo they'd picked up and delivered in the Djeda system had gone far in terms of purchasing supplies and outfitting the ship. But they couldn't stay there. Menefry had a price on his head or something stupid like that.

Judit had done an amazing job tracking down another cargo for them to haul. According to Saxon, bargaining was her superpower.

This shipment might pay enough that there would even be a tiny bit of profit for the rest of them. They'd all signed contracts as ship's crew, agreeing to a profit-sharing model. When the ship made money, they made money.

Kim had come up with some outlandish items they could "acquire" for shipping. Judit had put the kibosh on all of that. Still, Basil had to remember to ask Kim about the details.

Was it actually possible to steal an entire museum? And really, who would buy such a thing?

When the timer on the 3-D printer dinged, Basil picked up the conduit and inched zir way into the secondary engineering room.

It looked much better now. Smelled better too. The reek of burned flesh and rubber had been replaced with, well to be honest, a rich algae scent. While one section of the dais that Eleanor, Gawain, and Abban stood frozen on was still open, the rest of it had finally been closed up. The walls continued to be a patchwork of silver and green conduit, but Basil was slowly replacing what was there with better pieces, like the gray tubbing zie held in zir hand.

Zie still longed to raise Masala back from the dead, just to punch zir lights out.

Why, *why*, had zie added an acidic nature to the algae? So that it ate through the tubes it ran in?

"Fin for your thoughts?" came Eleanor's quiet voice.

"I have more pipe for you," Basil said, holding up the conduit zie carried. Zie was never certain how much Eleanor and the others saw versus sensed. Zie knew some philosophy geeks who would love to spend hours debating that in terms of the Oligochuno.

Basil knew that what zie *saw* was different than what any of the other races could. It was also almost impossible to separate the sense of seeing from tasting and smelling. In fact, the Oligochuno tended to use a single word for all of that, merely calling it *awareness*.

"But?" Eleanor prompted when Basil didn't continue.

"But I'm unsure about making more of the original organic cooling material or not," Basil continued. "It's acidic. It's going to break down the conduit it's in, no matter what I make it out of." Normally, zie would have used some sort of glass structure, but strangely enough, metal wore down more slowly.

"You know we need that coolant in order to survive," Eleanor said.

"I'm sure I can—"

"No," Eleanor said firmly. "We use it as more than just coolant."

"Oh," Basil said. A horrific thought came to zim. "You don't eat it, do you?" Zie had wondered about how the coolant ran under the dais, bathing the "feet" of the three beings. Did they somehow suck out nutrients from it?

Eleanor's appealing laughter spilled out around zim. "No. But the organic component makes it more malleable for us."

Basil wasn't sure why that was important, but zie still said, "I see." Zie was pushing at the limits of zir understanding. Zie still didn't have a straight answer as to how Eleanor and the others communicated. Was it psychic? Or some other sense, that zie didn't possess?

"How about if I keep it organic, but add a more neutral fluid?" Basil asked.

"I suspect that you'll find that Masala didn't add the acidity as a leash," Eleanor stated. "It's a necessary growth component for the algae."

"I suppose you're right," Basil said with a sigh. "Still. I'm going to keep experimenting."

"You sound like Masala when you say that," Eleanor said softly.

Basil hoped that was a compliment.

Zie went to work replacing one of the older pipes containing the viscous fluid with the newer piece zie held in zir hand. Then zie was going to spend the rest of the afternoon combing through Eleanor's code, removing the last of the "leashes" that Masala had programmed in, to keep the ship returning to their now destroyed base.

There had been some irregularities in the code that zie had to clean up. And once they reached the next station, zie could finally do the thing that zie had been looking forward to.

Go outside the ship and actually look at the secondary engines.

Humming, Basil continued in zir work, confident that zie could make it all right in the end.

CHAPTER 15

JUDIT

"*Mi a fenének!*" Judit muttered when she saw the station in the Gamor system that they were heading to. She was sitting in the main helm of the ship with Saxon. They had just exited the hyperspace gate.

It was another ancient space station, like *Atwak*. Except this time, instead of being a bunch of boxes of different sizes thrown together then attached, it was disks.

Who in their right mind would not only stack disks one on top of another, but also then have them on their side? It looked like a one-armed beast, with the main body being the disks that were stacked, then a long thin section that was the arm for the perpendicular disks.

She should have known that the Bantel wouldn't have a regular space station. Just as they didn't do normal colors.

Why had she allowed Kim to talk them into coming here? Oh yeah, that's right. Because Menefry had been too busy working on his own, personal salvation to get much good information about the price that might be on all their heads.

Everyone else had used a fake identity on the *Atwak*

station. Only Menefry had revealed his true name, and not just to his cousin, but to someone who actively hated him.

They weren't going back to the Djeda system anytime soon, that was for certain. Maybe ever. Even though that first cargo trip had been kind of sweet, transporting religious delicacies for the next big festival from one section of the system to the next. Menefry's cousin had paid well for a fast trip with cargo in a controlled environment.

It had been an easy haul. This next one would hopefully be the same.

Except it was a Bantel system. Judit couldn't quite shake the memory of what had happened the last time she'd been in a Bantel system, how she'd been set up for smuggling.

This time, there wasn't a Fran or an Arthur to come riding in and save her.

"I take it you don't approve of the, um, aesthetics of the *Gery* space station?" Saxon asked from where he was seated beside her.

Judit just glared at him. "Who builds a station like that?" she asked waving her hand in the general direction of the screen displaying the station.

"Obviously, the Bantel do," Saxon observed dryly. "I suppose, since they couldn't agree on what outlandish colors to paint the exterior, they decided to play with shapes instead."

"I would have thought that Arthur and his golden *Camelot* would have inspired them more," Judit grumbled.

"It may have," Saxon said. "Or perhaps because they didn't want to take the time repainting the exterior every month, they chose a more permanent oddity to focus on."

Judit rolled her eyes at him. Sure, he was trying to be diplomatic. She still didn't like it.

"Just be careful when we get there," she told him. "You

remember what happened the last time we were on a Bantel station."

"I will be," Saxon said, nodding. "You be careful as well."

"Yeah," Judit said. "I just hope that we're doing the right thing, trusting that Kim can get us more information about our current status, as well as *Eleanor's*. If any of the other ships survived."

The Bantel had been working hard at being more of a team player. Judit appreciated her effort. Even some of her dirty jokes had been funny. Why she had so many that she felt she needed to share with Judit, Judit would never know.

"I understand that Kim can get on your nerves sometimes." Saxon paused, then chuckled. "Okay, so possibly she gets on all of our nerves occasionally. I can't help but believe that she has the best of intentions though."

Judit shook her head. "I still don't trust her."

"What does she have to do in order to earn your trust?" Saxon asked seriously.

Judit opened her mouth then shut it again. She had no idea.

Saxon nodded. "You may want to think on that, my dear," he said. "Determine what she could do. Because like it or not, this crew will be together for a while. A long run, if you will."

Judit shifted uncomfortably on her pilot's couch. She knew she'd get homicidal if she was forced to be on this ship, day in and day out, with these people, no matter how much she might like them. Doing short runs between systems suited her much better.

Still, Saxon was correct. They were all in this together, as if they were making a long run. At least until they could ensure that they'd each have a future individually.

CHAPTER 16

MENEFRY

Menefry helped Saxon and Basil with offloading the last of the cargo, then found himself at loose ends. Saxon and Judit were going to find them another shipment to carry. Basil was preparing for his EVA, to go get a good look at the secondary engines. Kim was off having her own adventures. She was the only one who knew people on this station, though she promised to be careful.

Besides, the people she knew were supposedly thieves and fences, not necessarily the type to cooperate with the Cartel.

Menefry didn't know anyone. He was honestly still bruised and sore from the beating he'd taken back on *Atwak*. While he spent time stretching every day, he wasn't training at this point. He needed to heal, and even he knew that.

His main job on the ship was to protect the crew.

As Judit had Saxon to protect her, and Basil had Eleanor, Menefry decided to follow Kim, to make sure that she would be all right.

The *Gery* station was actually much more, well, *normal* than Menefry had been expecting. The interior reminded him of a Human station. Not that there was anything wrong with Human stations. It was just that…all the walls were the same color, an off-white that always looked dingy. And the floors tended to be hard steel and noisy. The lights, too, left much to be desired, too dim for Menefry's taste, though he understood that the Bantel, with their larger eyes, needed less light. Plus, the majority of the station was built to Bantel size, every place outside the areas where the other races were expected to be. Which meant that Menefry couldn't even stand upright in places.

In addition, there were no colorful statues. The scent of incense didn't linger in the air. He couldn't hear prayers in the background. It was cooler as well.

And though he'd known better, he'd still expected more outlandish colors or textures.

The Bantel, on the other hand, didn't disappoint. Menefry couldn't even name the colors he was seeing. It was a kaleidoscope of textures, fabrics, and scales. Fortunately, as he was so much taller, it felt like walking through a particularly colorful river in the parts that were more crowded.

Menefry hadn't bothered telling the rest of the crew that he had programmed his i-stick to be able to track their i-sticks. Eleanor had helped him do it, as she, too, wanted to keep the crew safe.

So he stayed well behind Kim as she ambled through the main ring of the station, past the market closest to where they'd parked *Eleanor*, through the long main hallway filled with more somber business fronts that offered insurance, health care, attorneys, and so on, and then into the next market section.

They were in one of the parts that Menefry thought of as vertical, as opposed to the horizontal stack of rings off to the side. The Bantel had set up an amusement park between the two sections, where the rides and games all played with the gravity shifts.

Though Menefry knew that Judit hadn't approved of the layout of the station, he knew that for some, the Path of Laughter was their highest calling.

Kim appeared to have settled into a café in the market, situated in the far corner. Menefry paused, not wanting to get close enough for her to see him. He spied a shop run by a Khanvassa, and ducked in there.

Menefry paused at the entrance, breathing in the sweet perfume of the Goddess's incense. A proper statue dedicated to her stood above the tiny counter on the left side, with her left limbs reaching up for luck and her right limbs stretched down to give it to those who properly worshiped at her feet.

The Bantel shops tended to feel empty, with broad clear aisles and tasteful lighting. It didn't make sense to Menefry that each shop only had a few items to sell, and you'd have to go to dozens to get everything you needed.

The shop he now stood in was properly full. The shelving units stood as tall as he was, jam-packed with barely enough space in the aisles for him to walk through. Just to the left of the door stood a small counter, crammed in on all sides with last-minute things that one might acquire. Menefry nodded in the direction of the shopkeeper standing there, then dove into the shop itself.

He was surprised that the shelves were still straight and not bowed due to the sheer amount of items clustered together on each. There were statues of the Goddess, of course, along with incense burners, prayer books, blessed pouches for carrying prayers, prayer mats, long strings of beads for counting prayers, specific candles for conducting various holiday celebrations.

And that was just the first aisle.

Specialized cooking gear for making Khanvassa delicacies filled much of the second, along with plates, glasses, and silverware that all the races could use. As Menefry explored, he found, well, everything that a person could need to set themself up in rooms here on the station.

The only thing lacking was clothing, but he suspected that if he asked the owner of the store about it, he'd know someone, or would have a cousin.

Menefry found himself drifting back to the front of the store and looking at the statues. He glanced at his i-stick. Kim hadn't moved.

In his rooms on *Camelot*, of course Menefry had had a statue dedicated to the Goddess. She stood with her center two limbs pressed together over her torso, as he would hold his hands in prayer position. The top two limbs reached up and away, the bottom two reached down and back.

It was the position of the Goddess mediating between the families, to bring peace to all sides of an argument, to intercede between warring factions.

That statue had meant a lot to Menefry when he'd first arrived at *Camelot*, and had been working on his penitence, praying for forgiveness between himself and his friends and family.

He didn't have a small statue of the Goddess on *Eleanor*. He'd planned on picking one up at *Atwak*, and hadn't had the time.

Maybe he could get one now, though…

Menefry looked at the smaller statues, each the length of his palm and fingers, and decided he needed something slightly bigger. The next size up were about the length of his forearm. What message did he need in his life?

Kim had suggested that he work on forgiveness of himself. But what did that actually mean? To forgive himself for falling in love with Arwenphtat in the first place? Forgive himself for trouncing his best friend Kemere so hard that he ended up in hospital? Forgive himself for all the pain and anguish he'd caused his family by being sentenced to jail?

There were other things that Menefry needed to forgive himself for as well. He just wasn't sure he was ready.

"Did you have any questions?" came the jovial voice from behind the counter.

Menefry turned and looked at the Khanvassa standing there. He was definitely older, his dark eyes faded and the edges of his shell thinned with age. His mandibles hung looser as well. He probably didn't have good control of them, and would be a messy eater who would get messier as he aged. He wore a yellow vest that was so bright that the Bantel would have approved of it. The nametag he wore stated, "Salo."

"I live on a spaceship now," Menefry admitted. "I need a statue for my rooms."

"The Goddess Brings Luck is a very popular statue with spacers," Salo said.

Menefry shook his head. "It isn't luck that I'm seeking." Not that he couldn't use more luck, but really, that wasn't in his prayers at the time.

"One of the mediation statues, then?" Salo suggested. "To ensure peace among your crewmates and your customers?"

Menefry turned to look at the statues that suggested prayer and peace. Though they were the most graceful of the stock that the merchant carried, none of them sang to him.

He was about to go when Salo said, "I have just the thing for you."

Menefry walked up to the front counter. It was really just an opening, as shelves stood on either side as well as across the top of the space, filled with lighters, small bottles, tiny screwdriver sets, electronic parts, many types of holders for different sizes of i-sticks, and more.

Salo reached under his counter and pulled up a status of the Goddess that Menefry had rarely seen. Her limbs stretched out all around her, none of them straight, but waving. She was painted in the traditional black. Gold fabric wafted around her, draped across her torso between her arms.

"The Goddess in Flux," Salo announced. "When she is in between things, in between tasks. She is moving from one step to the next, but hasn't arrived there yet."

Menefry noticed that indeed, she was standing only on one single limb. A second was poised as if to take the next step.

Yes. Exactly. This was what he had in mind. Not static, but moving. Not dancing, but progressing.

"How much?" Menefry asked.

He instantly regretted being on his own, without Judit, based on the gleam in Salo's eye.

IN THE END, Menefry thought he'd gotten a good bargain, though he knew that Judit could have done better. Salo carefully wrapped the Goddess's statue in the traditional bright green paper, as well as tied it with red ribbons, for luck. While the statue was acclimating to her new niche, Menefry would hang the ribbons from her hands. If the ribbons fell, he would know that she wasn't happy, and that he needed to find a new location for her.

With a happy sigh, Menefry left the shop and stepped back into the main hallway. He checked his i-stick. Kim was still at the café in the corner of the market.

As there were sure to be other Khanvassa in the area due to the excellent everything shop, he felt more confident. He strolled through the market on the opposite side, away from where Kim sat, engrossed in conversation with two other Bantel.

Good. She was making progress.

He still didn't let her see him.

Once the three of them had finished their meeting, the two slipped away and Kim remained, drinking some sort of fruit drink, glowing with an apparent sense of satisfaction.

Or perhaps that was just the amazing purple tint of her skin, matched with a red shirt that made the eye bleed a little.

Menefry decided, on a whim, to follow the two who had been meeting with Kim. Fortunately, they stayed in the main part of the station and didn't immediately dive into a Bantel section where Menefry couldn't have followed them.

They didn't go far from the market. However, they didn't step into a known shop or building.

Instead, they stepped into an unmarked access hatch of the station itself. The door wasn't necessarily hidden, but it wasn't obvious either.

Then a pair of Cartel guards walked out through the same door. They were both Bantel, both dressed in a single color of blue, with pale green and pink skin.

Had the two Menefry had been trailing just been caught going into someplace they shouldn't?

An office worker went in next. He would bet that she worked in customs given the subdued hue of her skin, as well as the Cartel blue outfit she wore.

Menefry thought that one of the original pair of Bantel came back out. He wasn't certain, but surely not that many of the Bantel had that particular pattern of red and black checked skin.

And that one held open the door for another guard dressed in Cartel blue to pass through.

Surely Kim hadn't been knowingly meeting with the Cartel? Were these just two some sort of spy, who had lied to Kim about their background?

Menefry didn't know what sort of game Kim was playing. All he knew was that he didn't like it.

CHAPTER 17

BASIL

Basil liked the EVA suit that Judit had found. Of course, zie would have preferred a life pod, basically, a miniaturized spaceship that zie could have flown around. However, those tended to be toys for rich people, not working suits.

Zie had tested both zir suit as well as hers, not finding any leaks or serious system issues. Zir helmet was not original to that particular suit: It was a much newer piece of equipment, for which zie was grateful.

The suit came with two permanent arms and had hookups where zie could add another four. When zie could afford it, zie would add at least one more. The gloves were configurable in terms of the number of fingers. Zie stuck with the basic three fingers and large opposable thumb. Again, when zie could afford it, zie would like to add sensors to the fingertips so zie could get better readings even in space.

Basil planned on starting with a scouting mission, to get a good look at the secondary engines. Zie had a good recording system in the newer helmet that would capture everything zie saw, including ranges outside of "normal" vision. Zie would pipe that recording directly to Eleanor, so that she got a really good look at her secondary engines as well.

Zie carried a small toolkit attached to zir suit, just in case there was an obvious issue that zie could easily fix. Or, as was likely to be the case, zie had to remove "shielding" from the engines, panels that didn't so much protect the engines as hide them.

Eleanor had several airlocks. Basil used the one at the back of the ship, in the engine room.

Though Basil had been in the engine room itself many times before, zie was always amazed at how *big* the room was. It was at least two stories tall, the entire width of the ship wide, and mostly empty. Zie used a ramp to get from the top level down to the base level, inching across the floor. The two tubes holding the main engines rose up on either side, covered in readouts that zie could tell at a glance were all normal. A soft hum filled the room, that zie could not only hear but feel along the segments of zir tail, yet another reassurance that all was well. It was always cooler in here, though neither the engines nor the equipment needed it that way. It was just a matter of convention.

At the very back of the engine room, on the far wall, stood an airlock. That was normal for most ships—to give easier access to the engines that stuck out the back. On even bigger ships, there were two airlocks, one beside either engine.

The airlock was the standard design, made from white material that stood out from the industrial gray walls of the rest of the engine room. Basil would bet that Arthur had wanted to do something fancy down here, but Masala had put zir tail down.

A wheel in the center of the door locked and unlocked it. While the wheel was small enough that a Bantel could easily use it, the door itself was tall and broad enough for a Khanvassa in an EVA suit to walk through without either turning sideways or bowing their head. Large lights along the right side of the door indicated the airlock's status: green for go, gray for waiting, and red for stop. Humans had originally used yellow to indicate waiting, but it turned out that color didn't register well with the Bantel, whose systems had used yellow for go for centuries before first contact.

Basil opened the interior door of the airlock and inched carefully into the airlock itself. It was a small room, really only big enough for two Humans or one Khanvassa. The door out to space had a large portal window in it that went from the top of the door almost to the center of it. At first, Basil thought it was a bit extravagant, then zie realized the window would be accessible for a Bantel as well as a Yu'udir.

Zie hooked a line from zir suit to the interior of the airlock, just inside the door, then tested both ends, to make sure that zie was firmly attached. Though the airlock was supposed to gradually release pressure, zie didn't want to accidentally be blown out into space.

Was the suit actually space-ready? Zie had tested it to the best of zir ability.

Here went nothing.

Zie spoke into the suit, linked directly to Eleanor, "Getting ready to leave the ship now."

"I know. Good luck," came her warm voice.

After taking another deep breath, zie flipped open the safety panel, then pressed the large red button that started the process to open the airlock.

"Depressurizing," came the mechanical voice that was the ship's main computer, not Eleanor.

Zie felt zir tail lift off the floor as the vacuum of space took hold.

After an interminable time with alarms sounding, warning of imminent exposure, the door finally opened.

Quiet descended. The velvet of the night awaited zim.

Basil gave an expert wiggle and propelled zieself out of the airlock. Zie kept the door open, but zie still swapped zir hook from the inside of the ship to the outside.

Eleanor was parked with her side to the space station. It stood to Basil's right. This close, all zie could see was the solid ring they were attached to, though if zie looked up or down, zie could see many more rings. They were too far away to see the side arm. Basil intended to visit the amusement park that connected the two before they left. Not because it sounded like fun, no, Basil was far too serious for that. But for the scientific study of how they gamified the use of gravity.

Really. Or at least that was what zie told zieself.

Basil grabbed one of the handy rungs attached to the side of the ship, then propelled zieself down, underneath the ship itself.

From the top, *Eleanor* had a compact design. But from the side, she was a solid mass of cargo holds. It took time for Basil to descend past the main engines, down the huge hold, finally reaching the bottom of the ship.

As zie had expected, panels covered the bottom of the ship, hiding what had to be the secondary engines. It was easy to tell which were actual shielding for the ship and which were merely decorative panels: the panels all had accessible bolts, while the shielding was riveted together. Plus, the panels were smaller than the shielding, each piece of it being between one to two meters square.

Basil paused for a moment, floating, examining everything zie saw. There were the usual nicks and scratches from being in space but no burn marks or any damage that looked as though it might threaten the integrity of the hull.

"Looking beautiful," Basil reassured Eleanor as zie got out zir ratchet set.

Of course, none of the sockets zie had matched the bolt heads. While the rest of the universe ran on metric, Masala had probably invented a new scheme and had specially printed tools for accessing the panels, just as a security measure. Or to be an ass.

Fortunately, Basil had come prepared. From the corner of zir tool case, zie pulled out a small piece of a pliable rubber-like substance that could withstand the coldness of space. Zie then got out zir ratchet, attached the biggest socket to it, then stuffed a piece of the rubber inside it. The rubber would stay malleable for a short while, fitting around to the shape of the bolthead zie pressed the socket onto. After it hardened, zie would have a socket that would perfectly match the boltheads of the access panel.

Basil didn't have a lot of upper body strength, unlike a Human or a Yu'udir. While zie could grow stronger arms, there was a limit to what zie could do. The bolts were stiff and didn't want to turn. It was extra special trying to have any sort of leverage in zero G.

However, with some luck and a lot of cursing (Basil even used some of the Hungarian zie had picked up from Judit) zie managed to get a single access plate off.

Basil didn't know what zie had been expecting. Possibly something normal, like a regular atomic engine. Knowing Arthur, maybe even a combustion engine or a steam engine. But zie had figured that it would be something that resembled an engine.

Instead, zie was faced with tubes and more tubes, filling the entire meter-square section zie could see. Some were square and flat, others were round. All of them were about fifteen centimeters in diameter. They glowed with an eerie blue-white light that came and went, like a sluggish heartbeat. It didn't surprise zie that they looked organic in nature.

If only they weren't parked outside of a space station! Zie would have gladly grown a second tail to be in a dry dock so that zie could properly inspect the material the tubes were made out of.

Basil knew that zie wasn't seeing the entire engine, but just a small section of it. Where were the moving parts? Where was the power source? How did this engine even work?

Zie was just going to have to come back out here again, probably with Judit, as she was the only other person on the ship with an EVA suit. They were going to have to take off more of the panels, see if they could get enough of a picture to understand what they were seeing.

Zie remembered the story of a group of blind Humans trying to describe an elephant. They each only "saw" their section, be it a foot, a tail, or a trunk.

With a single access panel open, all Basil could see was possibly the intestines of the engine, or an arm, or maybe even its hair, not the entire beast itself.

Basil sighed and reattached the bolts. Zie would make a couple of sockets that would fit the bolt heads while zie waited for Judit to return to the ship, then the pair of them could do some additional exploring.

Hopefully, zie would then be up to the challenge of putting all the pieces of the puzzle of the secondary engines together.

CHAPTER 18

KIM

"Of *course* the people I was meeting were Cartel agents!" Kim sputtered.

Really, what did Menefry expect?

"Duh!" Kim added. "How else are we going to find out what the Cartel knows about us?"

They sat in what he considered his "office," that desert conference room. She could tell that he'd bumped the temperature up, as well as the gravity. It made the place a real downer, in more ways than one. Fortunately, she was dressed in lime green shorts that helped to liven up the place. Her black-and-white striped top may have looked a little plain in comparison, except that the edges of each black stripe were done in gorgeous black sequins that glittered and caught the light every time she moved. She'd colored her skin that day a lovely tan that didn't quite go with the décor of the room, but it wasn't too bad. And her eyes matched the red of the sunset that was just ending.

At least Menefry hadn't started burning that stinky incense that had permeated the *Atwak* station. Or maybe he had tried and Judit had put her foot down.

Kim was surprised that he hadn't put up a statue to the Goddess here in the conference room, particularly given how many she'd seen at the station. Then again, while Menefry was religious, he wasn't orthodox. She'd only been able to listen to his private prayers a couple of times, before he'd rerouted her spying software. They'd been full of asking for redemption, of guilt and remorse.

"Meeting with the Cartel is dangerous," Menefry finally said quietly.

"No more so than flying around in a stolen, experimental spaceship," Kim countered. "Particularly one that's based on actual aliens."

"Point," Menefry said with a nod. "However, getting in touch with the Cartel is a huge risk. You should have consulted with us first."

"Like you did when we were on *Atwak*?" Kim asked innocently. Well, innocently enough. "Before you gave out your real name? Unlike the rest of us, who are still operating under aliases?"

"That was a mistake," Menefry said. "And I am sorry about that. Truly, I am."

Kim couldn't help but roll her eyes at that. All that meant was that the sorry bastard had spent additional time flat on his back begging for even more forgiveness.

"My meeting with these two was *not* a mistake," Kim said. "I have more than one alias that I'm using, so they don't know who I actually am. Plus, these two were vouched for by a different contact. They'll stay bought."

Though that might have been stretching the truth. What her contact had said about the Cartel agents was that you had to make sure the bribe was big enough so that they would stay bought. Otherwise, they might sell you out.

What could be bigger than hinting about a special spaceship for sale?

Not that Kim would sell *Eleanor* out from under the rest of the crew. She would have to make sure that everyone would be provided for before she stole the ship. That much she promised herself.

"It is my responsibility to make sure that all of the crew are protected and kept safe," Menefry said.

"So you didn't just happen to be following me?" Kim said. "Or if you were, it was for my own good?"

Menefry tilted his head from one side to the other. "I…I want to make sure no harm comes to you." Then he straightened up on his chair. "But also know that I consider *Eleanor* a member of the crew as well. I won't allow any harm to come to her, either."

"It's a good thing that I got my sister's back, then, isn't it?" Kim said. At his confused look, which honestly was kind of adorable, with the slack pincers and wide brown eyes, she added, "Eleanor could be considered a sister to all of us, couldn't she?"

Menefry brightened up considerably at that. "Yes, yes she could be."

"And I wouldn't turn my sister into the Cartel, rest assured," Kim said.

No, she'd have to find a really rich buyer for *Eleanor*. Only the best for her sister. Or something like that.

"All right," Menefry said slowly, nodding.

Kim stood up. Really, this place was just a little too warm for her tastes. Not that she was nervous or anything. Besides, her neck ruff hid her "sweat" glands. No one would be able to tell that she was getting hot around the collar. They'd have to get really close to be able to see the tell-tale white crystals that the skin beneath her scales shed.

"Don't be following me," Kim said, pointing at him. "I'm serious. I can take care of myself."

"Of course," Menefry said, spreading his arms wide.

Kim rolled her eyes. She recognized that gesture. It was the same as some of the shopkeepers on *Atwak* station had used. It meant that the issue was no longer in their hands but in the arms of the Goddess.

Kinda creepy.

It also meant that Menefry was going to follow her around on this station regardless of what she said.

Luckily, it was a Bantel station.

And Kim could literally blend into the walls if she wanted to.

CHAPTER 19

SAXON

Not too far from the central marketplace where *Eleanor* was parked, Saxon found exactly the sort of pub that he was in the mood for.

It wasn't the sort of place that he'd feel comfortable bringing Judit to. First of all, it was primarily a Yu'udir bar. While they would of course make accommodations for all the races, it was deliberately built to not fit the others. The tables, chairs, and bar were all the appropriate height and sturdiness for a Yu'udir. Highchairs and booster seats were available, but they were stacked up against the side of the bar and looked rarely used.

It was also blessedly cool inside, and the air had been scented with a deliberate hint of ice and snow, that kind of stale smell that you got in a place where nothing was growing for kilometers. Saxon found it surprisingly comforting.

The walls as well as the bar were all done in a faux flagstone, gray with hints of gold running through it. It felt like a hardy, rustic place, despite all the modern conveniences that were built in. However, it was yet another reason why he'd never bring Judit here: all those harsh edges for her to run into. Particularly along the sides of the bar. She'd come back a mass of bruises. Not that his captain wasn't graceful. She just didn't always pay attention to her surroundings when she was in a hurry.

As expected, he found only other Yu'udir inside. A group of three was sitting at one of the dozen tables spread across the floor, dressed as laborers in thick denim vests and heavily drinking based on the number of empty pints already sitting at their table. A couple of other tables had people sitting and chatting quietly, while a few individuals sat up at the bar.

Saxon contained his sigh when he saw all the screens lined up above the bar, playing old games of a Yu'udir sport that the Humans called *hurling*. Except that the Yu'udir version involved heavy personal contact and was played on a field of snow and ice.

A sports bar. Of course, he should have expected that. Most of the Yu'udir who came through this station would be muscle and cargo haulers.

At least the screens were not all blaring. As Saxon approached the bar, he saw that in order to hear a particular match you'd have to pay for the code to listen to it.

The barkeep was an older Yu'udir, her white hair thinning and grown coarse in places, and her blue eyes faded. She still stood tall and proud behind her bar, with strong biceps, probably from hauling supplies into her pub. The vest she wore was a particularly searing shade of green that left Saxon questioning her taste level. However, he'd seen excellent reviews of the beer served here, particularly the porter. He ordered a pint of that, along with some fried *ullanti* strips—a delicacy that Judit declared tasted like poorly done skirt steak. She just didn't have the teeth necessary for tearing apart the flesh of her enemies. She'd probably just try to curse the hide off one.

While waiting for his order, Saxon noticed a replica of

Camelot hanging above the small array of bottles on the wall behind the bar, probably sixty centimeters long. It hung like a golden dream, just out of reach.

"You ever get there?" the barkeep asked, noticing what had caught his attention. Her name, according to her nametag, was Tillie. The porter she handed Saxon was a dark, rich looking color with a minor amount of foam. It smelled heavenly.

"Yes. A couple of times," Saxon said. He shook his head. "Was supposed to make it for the birthday party this year."

"Lucky you missed it, then," Tillie said solemnly. "I heard that there wasn't any warning before the asteroid hit."

"Asteroid?" Saxon said, curious. Was that the official reason being given for how the station got destroyed?

Tillie shrugged as well as tilted her head from side to side. "Yeah, I don't believe that either. Too many warning systems would have had to be sabotaged in order for something of that magnitude to make it through. At least the Khanvassa aren't claiming that it was an Act of the Goddess or something stupid."

"What do you believe happened?" Saxon asked as he took a sip of the porter. Gods, that was lovely. Smooth, with just the perfect amount of bitter right at the very end.

Tillie snorted. "Cartel blew it up," she said bluntly. "Couldn't afford to allow a freethinker like Arthur to stick around."

Saxon paused, then lifted his glass toward *Camelot*. "To Arthur," he said softly.

"You might not want to do too much of that," Tillie said. "Particularly on a Cartel station like this one."

"Not approved of by the powers that be?" Saxon said with just the hint of a growl.

"Might get you some hard questioning, like that poor bastard they hauled in last week," Tillie said. She leaned across the bar and added, "He claimed that his ship was just leaving *Camelot* and saw the explosion. It wasn't an asteroid, at least not according to him. Looked as though thousands of charges went off all at once along all the rings."

Saxon felt his throat go dry, despite the lovely brew he'd been sipping. "Sabotage," he growled.

"Just keep that under your vest for now," Tillie warned.

Saxon stayed standing at the bar while he contemplated the destruction of *Camelot*. How would he have gone about doing it? Not as though he was a demolition expert. He might have to check with Menefry about that, or possibly Basil would have a better idea.

"Would take a team to plant that many explosives," Saxon said after a few moments.

"Naw, just a single dedicated enhanced type," Tillie said, shaking her head. "Or at least that's who I would have hired. Not that I'm in the habit of hiring assassins or terrorists."

"Just one person?" Saxon said, trying to imagine it.

"Would take a week, maybe ten days, of constant EVA," Tillie said. "And thousands of tiny charges."

"You've thought this through," Saxon said, narrowing his eyes at Tillie.

Tillie shrugged and tilted her head from side to side again. "Haven't you? Hasn't every Yu'udir in this place?"

"And shall the hall of the dead
Unleash its angry horde
Upon all the righteous suspects
Who cry of how they've been wronged?"

Saxon quoted.

"Aye, you've got it there," Tillie said, nodding with approval. "Though I doubt an angry enough horde could be gathered anymore. All they took was a dream. Nothing more."

Saxon took his *ullanti* strips and his excellent porter and went to sit at a corner table when Tillie served another client.

She might be right. The more time that passed after the death of Arthur and *Camelot*, the less likely he'd be able to raise an angry horde and have his revenge.

Still, Arthur and the dream of *Camelot* deserved more than just a passing mention in history. He raised his glass once more in the direction of the image of *Camelot* over the bar while he considered Tillie's words.

As well as how to go about finding a single assassin who'd committed the largest crime of his generation.

———

SAXON WAS on his way back to the station with a better idea of how to focus his searches when he saw Kim just ahead of him.

Or at least he thought it was Kim. He'd seen her earlier, and had remarked on the particular turquoise color of her skin. While Bantels did tend to be colorful, he hadn't seen any other in quite the same outfit.

The hallway he walked along was crowded, with Bantel filling the entire space. Luckily, he was at least a head taller than most of the people who walked along.

It reminded him of a festival, with all the bright colors and chipper, happy people. He knew that the Bantel's attitude tended to unnerve Judit but he generally didn't mind it. It did make him watch his i-stick a bit more closely, as he suspected a pickpocket wouldn't stand out in such a crowd.

Now, where had Kim gotten to? She was just ahead.

No, wait. She was near the edge of the hallway, just before it opened out onto one of the marketplaces.

Two Human guards emerged from a hidden doorway. If Saxon hadn't been paying particular attention, he might not have noticed them, how they picked up the smaller Bantel by the arms and hustled her off, back behind the walls of the station.

She'd been taken.

No one else appeared to notice a thing. Or perhaps they'd been trained to not notice, particularly on, what had Tillie called it? A Cartel run station such as this one?

Saxon pushed his way through the crowd, hurrying past the door and back toward the ship.

He would need backup before he tried storming this particular castle gate.

CHAPTER 20

JUDIT

JUDIT SAT IN HER OFFICE, in the comfy chair at the back, looking out the window. At least she had the expanse of space to look out on, and not merely the ring of the station they were cozied up to.

It was almost soothing watching the ships fly to and away from the station. Almost. There was another part of Judit that was still on constant alert, afraid that one or more of those ships would suddenly divert from their expected trajectory and head straight for *Eleanor*, boxing her in so that they couldn't fly away.

It had been a depressing morning. While none of the crew were accessing the accounts associated with their true names, Basil had finally added some filters and forwarders so that they could at least access their email.

Despite her spam filters, her inbox was near to overflowing with junk. She'd ruthlessly deleted most of it, nearly wiping out a personal message from her older brother Gábor.

Judit was the second oldest in her family, with one older brother, then a younger brother and sister. She and Gábor had always done things together, while her younger siblings had formed their own bond. It had frequently been one set against the other.

She hadn't gone back to Záhony space station in three years, though she did occasionally send Gábor a name day greetings, when she remembered.

When Judit had signed up for Arthur's program, she'd had to redo her will, and had gotten in touch with Gábor. They'd exchanged a few emails at that time, catching up. She'd ended up leaving everything to his two kids.

The others could support themselves as far as she was concerned. She'd never been close to them, or them to her.

The email she'd nearly deleted turned out to be a live recording of Gábor. He'd received the notification that she'd died when the space station *Camelot* had been destroyed.

The video was Gábor's way of dealing with the grief, which was to basically deny it. He said that he figured she was too stubborn to die that way, that instead, she was meant to blow herself up spectacularly long after he'd gone, doing something stupid, not by being in the wrong place at the wrong time.

He'd ended the piece by reading out loud one of her favorite poems, a dark, dismal piece from the Communist era, about how black the day, the sun, everything was.

Fekete a nap...

Which put Judit in an even fouler mood.

Could she tell her brother that she was still alive? Would that put him, or more importantly, his kids, at peril?

No, better to disappear, and stay gone, if for nothing else, the incredibly handsome payout that Arthur's insurance company was still honoring.

Now, she just had to stay alive, which meant worrying

about an experimental spaceship that was expected to break down regularly, the Cartel still potentially coming after them, and a whole slew of other things.

Basil appeared at her door before she could dive down deeper into her paranoia.

"Did you look at the recording I made during my EVA?" zie asked even as zie crossed the threshold of her office.

"I did," Judit said slowly. She sighed and stood, then went to stand behind her "work" desk.

"When are we going to do the next EVA?" Basil asked expectantly.

"I don't know," Judit said. She slid out her desk chair and sat down in it, instantly regretting the action since she'd left her coffee back next to her comfy chair.

She could tell that Basil was disappointed in her answer. Zie had probably expected her to already be in her EVA suit and waiting for zim to go.

She contained her sigh, telling herself that this was a potential teaching moment and she needed to use it as such.

Though when the *franc* had she become the functioning adult to this merry band?

"What does Eleanor think of the recording?" Judit said pointedly.

"Uhm…" was all the reply she got.

"Or Gawain? Or Abban?" she pressed.

A Human or Bantel would be shifting uncomfortably in their chair about this time. An Oligochuno just got stiffer, as if the segments that made up zir torso shifted closer together.

"While I'm glad that you are asking for my help, and I will happily give it, I would check with those who might actually *know* something first," Judit said. Okay, so possibly a bit heatedly.

The Oligochuno didn't sigh. Basil did appear to take a deep breath, zir sides flexing slightly. "You're right."

"Should we ask them now?" Judit said sweetly.

"Please," Basil replied.

"Eleanor?" Judit called out, knowing that the ship was always listening. "Have you reviewed the recording that Basil made?"

"I have," Eleanor said. She at least sounded amused and not angry about being left out. "I have no idea what to make of it."

"But?" Judit pressed. "What about Gawain? Or Abban?"

"Gawain says that the center of the secondary engines is the only section that he activates," Eleanor continued. "And he says those parts, at least according to his understanding, are very similar to the standard engine design. And are all working correctly."

"What about Abban?" Basil piped up.

"Abban is the one who uses the rest of the structure," Eleanor replied.

Judit wasn't certain why Eleanor sounded reluctant. Was it just out of habit? The ship had been leashed pretty thoroughly by Masala and Arthur so it wouldn't accidentally give away any secrets. Or was there something else that she wanted to hide?

"What is the rest of the structure?" Judit said. "Is it an engine?"

"No," Abban suddenly said.

Judit was surprised. Zie rarely spoke up except for when they were accessing hyperspace.

"It is a representation," Abban said. "A model."

"A model of what?" Basil said, though Judit was already nodding, understanding what Abban was getting at.

"Of hyperspace," Abban said. "Very small model. It helps us dig in and out of tunnels."

Judit felt the enormity of what Abban was saying fill the

space of her office. It was as if the air had suddenly grown thick and viscous.

"Are any parts of the model broken at this time?" Judit asked after a moment while Basil also absorbed the possibilities of what Abban had said.

"Yes," Abban said. She could hear the relief in zir voice. "I will give you a diagram."

Judit opened her mouth then closed it again. How in *isten neve* were they supposed to fix a model of hyperspace? Even a small one?

"Hologram is ready now," Eleanor said.

Judit dutifully reached over to her desk console and pressed the play button that would bring up a hologram.

The usual representation of hyperspace was a round, semi-transparent ball with hundreds of points heading into the center and meeting there.

The hologram that sprang up above her desk only bore the slightest resemblance to that. Instead of a neat and tidy ball, it was a structure with a solid mass in the center and tentacles sprouting out in all directions. As the image rotated, Judit understood that each one of those tentacles was a hyperspace tunnel, particularly when she saw that many of them were doubled, indicating a tunnel going in either direction.

The model glowed with the same blue-white light of the secondary engine that Basil had recorded. It also seemed to have that same slow pulse of a heartbeat.

As they watched, the center of the model started expanding, pushing the tentacles out and apart. Instead of being about the size of a Human head, it was now the length of a typical Human arm, and growing.

"Do you see?" Eleanor asked.

When Basil didn't reply, Judit pointed to the dark spot

that was just above center and to port? Starboard? How the hell were they supposed to describe such a thing?

"Yes," Basil finally said. Zie sounded out of breath.

Was zie able to sense more about the model than Judit could see?

"I take it the 'top' of the model is toward the head of the ship?" Judit finally asked as the hologram shrank back down.

"It is," Eleanor said. "And that dark spot is on the starboard side."

"Thank you," Basil said. Zir voice was a whisper. "That was…incredible."

What had zie sensed?

"I'm not sure what you'll be able to do to fix it," Eleanor admitted. "The technology…we can't really explain it. Abban just uses it. I didn't even realize that the model Abban uses was replicated on the ship, as the second engine system."

"Do we need to go to Chonchu space next?" Judit asked. Since the core of *Eleanor* was based on those aliens, maybe they'd have an idea of how to fix it.

The sigh that Eleanor gave made Judit smile. Though she knew that she couldn't take the ship out drinking, she still had that impulse sometimes.

Take a sister out to a bar, let her drink herself silly enough that she'd actually let loose.

"I don't know," Eleanor said. "I would think going back there would be our last resort. No one knew what would happen to us if we were suddenly re-enmeshed with the hive mind. It was one of the reasons why Masala installed so many 'leashes' on our systems. So that we wouldn't suddenly be taken over in case we came into contact with one of our queens."

"I see," Basil said. Zie nodded. "Do you think there's any chance that any of the Chonchu scientists who were working on the project survived? That their notes may have been left behind in their home system?"

"That's possible," Eleanor said. "If any of them returned to the home world. Their work would have been shared, so that it wouldn't be lost. Not unless all the queens were wiped out again."

That was another reason why they shouldn't go back to the Chonchu systems, particularly if they were being tracked by the Cartel. That might lead to more repercussions against the Chonchu.

"Okay," Judit said. "We'll table going back there for now. In the meanwhile, I suppose you want to go back out and try to see more of what's going on in this model?" Judit said looking at Basil.

"If you wouldn't mind," Basil replied mildly.

"All right," Judit said, pushing herself up. She walked back and grabbed her coffee, taking one last swig of it. It was still delightfully warm and good, but duty called. "Let's go see this thing."

Before Judit could cross her office again, Saxon showed up at her door, with Menefry in tow.

"Kim's been taken," he announced. "By the Cartel."

"And we must go rescue her," Menefry added. "Now."

Judit shook her head. Though the others couldn't hear it, the sound of a shoe dropping and landing on a floor in heavy gravity resounded in her imagination.

She calmly faced the others, who appeared to be on the edge of panicking. Needed to nip that in the bud first.

"It's going to be all right," she told them, keeping her voice soothing. "I already have a plan in mind."

CHAPTER 21

KIM

KIM HAD A REALLY bad feeling about this.

Mind you, probably anyone would at this point, having been hustled away from the main corridor of the space station by Cartel guards, then stuck in this awful room. First off, it was *cold* in here. It was worse than the icy conference room back on *Eleanor*. Kim sat on a steel chair that had probably been dragged out of a refrigerator. The steel table she was handcuffed to was cold as well. She'd been trying to fog it with her breath, watching the condensation spread, but that fun only lasted so long.

The next horrible part was just how dark the room was. She knew that the Humans kept their interrogation rooms starkly bright, so you couldn't hide anything.

It was supposed to encourage the truth, or something idiotic like that.

The Bantel understood that the power of darkness was stronger. While there was a single bright light shining down out of the ceiling just inside the stupidly locked door, the rest of the room was in shadows.

Particularly behind her.

Kim jumped every time the fans in the room kicked on. She found herself straining to hear, well, anything. Was there someone behind her? Another Bantel, blended perfectly into the darkness? She couldn't tell and it was making her a little crazy.

Crazier.

In response to the darkness, Kim had brightened up the turquoise of her skin, until it was practically neon. She didn't actually glow, but damn it, she was close. She couldn't change the colors of any of her clothes, so she just imagined that the yellow of her cute shorts was warm, like the sun, instead of cool, like lemon sorbet. Her top was a pretty pink, but imagining it to be redder wasn't working for her. Maybe purple? Like that lovely purple blanket she had back in her nest on *Eleanor*?

The ship. Kim contained her sigh. Okay, so maybe, *maybe*, she'd pressed her luck too far. It had just been going so well with her contacts! And she'd thought that the idea of perhaps having a special ship to sell would have kept them bought.

Seemed the Cartel had paid a higher price for their loyalty this time.

She wasn't sure how she was going to get out of this one. Her general sunny nature seemed to be failing her.

One way would be to give the Cartel *Eleanor*. However, that would abandon the crew to their "tender" mercies, and besides, there was no guarantee that she'd be able to get away afterward. No, they'd probably want to "rehabilitate" her (again) or some such nonsense.

There wasn't anyone she could call, though. No favors she could beg. She'd burned a lot more bridges than she'd realized when she'd been nabbed during the heist that originally brought her to the attention of Arthur and Fran.

Poor Fran. She rarely thought of him. It wasn't as if

they'd been dating or something dumb like that. They hadn't even had sex, though there, towards the end, they had sorta kinda been dancing around that.

No, thinking of Fran was definitely depressing, especially when she was already, well, here. In this stark, cold, interrogation room.

She stared over her shoulder again when she thought she heard a noise. Maybe the sound of someone subtlety shifting, their clothes not tight enough to mask the sound.

All she saw behind her was darkness.

Maybe whoever was in charge had just added noises to the room, to get someone like her to spook.

Yup. That had to be it. There wasn't an assassin just waiting behind her, ready to lop her head off the moment she said the wrong thing, made the wrong move.

Or gave up her friends.

CHAPTER 22

BASIL

"I've identified the location where they're probably holding her," Basil told the others as they gathered around the screen zie had projected on Judit's desk. They were all crowded around it. Saxon had joined Judit on "her" side, while Menefry crouched beside Basil to get a better look.

Zie hadn't been particularly surprised by Judit's proposal. It only made sense that she'd have a contingency in place in case someone got in trouble on one of the space stations they visited.

"It's a standard holding unit," Menefry announced, looking at the hoovering architectural plans. "There should be guards here, here, and here," he said, indicating intersections with one of his more delicate secondary arms.

"Really? That many guards?" Basil asked, surprised. "I would think they would have more automatic systems."

"They do have a lot of automatic systems," Menefry said. "Heat sensors, motion detectors, atmospheric controls. If you have a dedicated enough hacker, you can get around most, if not all of those." He paused, nodding. "While it's easy enough to bribe one guard, perhaps even two or three, a dozen or so makes it impossible to maintain secrecy. Someone is going to talk."

"Luckily we aren't trying to bribe anyone," Judit said dryly. "We're going in hot, coming out hotter. There's a good chance that we are burning this bridge but good. If anyone has any objections, speak now."

"Why are you doing this?" Saxon inquired in his most polite tones.

"What do you mean?" Judit said flatly.

"You and Kim are not necessarily the closest of crewmates," Saxon said.

Basil felt zir torso stiffen with embarrassment as Saxon went on.

"You barely tolerate her at times. You've said on more than one occasion that you do not trust the Bantel, any of them, including Kim. Why are you so hellbent on rescuing her? There isn't too much she can tell them about *Eleanor* or the rest of us. We could just slip away and disappear, come up with new identities, a new team if necessary. Why the big push?"

Judit nodded. "That's a fair question," she said slowly. "And you're right, I rarely see eye to eye with the Bantel. Ultimately, they're the ones who got us into this situation in the first place, putting contraband goods on my ship."

Interesting. Menefry stirred at that, as though he was just about to say something, but then thought the better of it.

"And while I may not agree with Kim a lot of the time, she's still a member of this crew."

She added a Hungarian phrase that Basil was going to have to look up later, but zie assumed that it translated roughly into, "*My* goddamned crew."

"If anyone is going to space a member of my crew for doing something as idiotic as turning us over to the Cartel, it's going to be me pressing the airlock button. And laughing the entire time," Judit assured them all. She paused, then added, "I think—I hope—that Kim wasn't turning us over. I figure she just did something stupid. Stupider than usual. I'd rather give her the benefit of the doubt, at least for now."

Basil found zieself suddenly more settled at Judit's words. Zie hadn't realized that she felt that strongly about them, that she had claimed them as hers. That she would fight for them, each and every one of them, when they screwed up, would come and rescue them if they got taken.

Zie assumed that Judit would have moved soil and stone if Saxon had been taken. That she felt the same about all of them warmed zir torso and steadied zir tail.

"So how do we get her out?" Menefry asked.

"We don't," Judit said with a wry smile. "We get them to bring her to us."

Basil inched slowly through the marketplace. Zie was certain that zie was being followed. However, there wasn't much zie could do about it. There were very few of the Oligochuno on the station.

The majority of the people on the station were either Bantel or Human. While Menefry and Saxon wouldn't necessarily blend in, at least every time they left the station there weren't hundreds of eyes staring at them.

Basil tried to make zieself look as important as possible. Instead of growing pockets along the sides of zir torso for all of zir instruments, zie had grown extra hands to hold them all.

As if putting zir tools into and dragging them out of pockets wasted too much time when there were more important matters.

Basil stopped at one of the first controls for the station

that zie came across. The Bantel didn't build their monitors into the walls like any normal race. No, all of their monitors stood on pedestals in the corners of various rooms. Sometimes they were protected in a plexiglass case, but most stood out in the open.

Zie understood why. Anything on the walls, anything at all, would represent a "challenge" to a Bantel. They would look at it and wonder how close could they get to mimicking it. It was why all the walls in the common areas of the station were monotone and gray. They were too "easy" for the Bantel.

Where was the fun in blending into a wall that anyone could, even a hatchling as young as one or two?

The first control was used to maintain and monitor lighting in this section. It really wasn't that central of a mechanism. However, Basil still puffed zieself up with importance as zie brought up one of zir tools and fiddled with the screen case on the monitor. Satisfied, zie nodded and moved onto the next one.

What the watchers didn't see was the secondary arm that sneaked out and placed a small device on the underside of the monitor, out of sight.

The device wouldn't do much on its own. However, Basil intended to plant many more. Together, they'd form a network that would piggyback on the existing lighting system.

It was part of the plan that Judit had come up with, a way of ensuring maximum chaos. It wasn't the main thrust of the plan, just one of the many mis-directions that she'd thought up.

Basil was very glad that Judit was on their side, that zie wasn't having to go against her. She had thought of damned near everything.

Not because she enjoyed doing such planning. No, but

because she always assumed the worst case going into any situation and she needed to have a plan to get out of it.

When Judit had brought up this portion of her plan, Saxon had talked about the scuttlebutt he'd heard, about how *Camelot* hadn't been brought down by a team, but possibly by a single person who'd planted thousands of little explosives.

Basil planted a few more devices in the area very close to where Kim was being held, until zie was confident that zie could kill the lights outside the security office.

Plus, no one was watching zim anymore. They'd all grown accustomed to zim in this area.

It meant that zie could move on to the next set of monitors.

The alarms.

CHAPTER 23

MENEFRY

THOUGH MENEFRY WOULD HAVE PREFERRED to do this part of the job on his own, Judit had insisted that Saxon go with him. There needed to be two of them to "seal" the deal, as it were.

He wasn't sure that he wanted to know how it was that she knew that. Or how she could locate the appropriate clothing for him and Saxon so quickly.

They were both wearing Cartel blue, though not full uniforms. Saxon wore a blue vest that he scratched at, complaining of the rough material. Menefry could sympathize: the shirt he was in felt like stiffly molded plastic, not cloth. And the pants were even worse. At least he'd been able to wear his own shoes.

They looked more like office workers than guards.

Mean office workers with an extra shell on their shoulders, who worked in a dangerous office that required the people there to carry a small arsenal of weapons with them at all times.

The paperwork that Basil had generated for them

wouldn't pass a serious inspection. They all knew that. They were risking their own shells to go and rescue Kim.

Still, Menefry had agreed with Judit's reasoning. Kim *was* one of theirs. She was becoming a friend, someone who you could trust to clean your gossamer wings and not rip them accidentally.

If Kim had turned on them, well, Judit wouldn't be the only one there at the airlock wishing the Bantel good riddance.

They used the i-stick that Basil had hacked for them, getting them past the first set of doors and into the front of the security office.

Menefry tried his best to look menacing, keeping his mandible flexed, as if just waiting to take a bite out of someone. Saxon's fur appeared to be standing on edge along the back of his neck. They walked into the front of the security office as if they owned the place.

The office looked exactly as Menefry had anticipated, though the walls were even more stark than usual. On top of the counter, a glass barrier separated the small, skinny reception area from the larger section behind. That barrier would be proof against most beam weapons. It might also be electrified, so that anyone trying to break through it would get themselves zapped pretty hard.

Most of the people in the front of the security section were merely office workers. They weren't actually guards. It wouldn't be difficult to go through the entire room and knock every single person out. However, it would be time consuming. The ones who Menefry hadn't gotten to yet would have been able to sound an alarm.

Deeper inside the section were the real guards. The ones with training, who might pose a threat to Menefry. Particularly since they'd have no compunction about stunning him from a distance.

"Who's in charge?" Saxon growled from the counter, slapping down the paperwork with a huge, heavy paw.

Menefry was surprised at how completely Saxon had transformed himself. Instead of coming across like a well-educated priest, he sounded like a laborer who'd walked in straight from the desert and hadn't even bothered brushing the sand from his shell.

Slowly, one of the Bantel got up from her desk. She had a Cartel blue shirt and pants, while her skin was a clashing light green and her eyes were a glowing purple. "Yes?" she said as she sauntered up. "Can I help you gentlemen?"

Menefry could practically hear Saxon rolling his eyes at her. "Gotta prisoner pickup," he said, shoving the paperwork at the Bantel.

She frowned, looking down at the papers. "You're early," she said.

"Boss pays extra if we're quick about it," Menefry said. He loosened his mandibles slightly and settled his shell back down on his back.

Let Saxon play the Goddess at war. Menefry could be the peacemaker.

"She hasn't been processed," the office worker said, looking up something on the screen hidden beneath the counter.

"Don't care," Saxon growled.

"We just need to get her back to the big man as soon as we can," Menefry said smoothly. He couldn't quite manage an eyeroll with his physiology. However, he did give the Bantel a wink with the eye that was furthest away from Saxon. "If you don't mind."

"I'll see what I can do," she said, turning back away.

As if on cue, Judit came barreling into the office. "Who's in charge?" she demanded.

Menefry stared at her. It was kind of difficult not to.

Judit normally never wore any makeup. Today, though, she'd outlined her lips in a bright red lipstick that made her look like a hungry predator. Her hair was sticking up all over her head, as if it, too, was about to attack. She'd changed into Cartel blue as well, though her outfit was quite a bit more refined than any of the office workers.

"Are you in charge?" Judit said rudely barging into the conversation he and Saxon had been having.

Saxon growled at her as a matter of course. Judit didn't even bother looking at him.

"I'm the office manager," the Bantel said.

"She's taking care of us first," Saxon said.

"Please," Menefry added.

The poor Bantel looked from Saxon to the obviously important Cartel member in front or her. "Joey?" she called, bringing a male Bantel who'd been sitting at his desk, looking as though he wanted to stay in the background and watch the show. "Can you take care of these gentlemen?"

Joey didn't look any more thrilled dealing with Saxon or Menefry. "We are in kind of a hurry," Menefry said, sounding more apologetic than ever.

Joey glanced at Menefry, at the still growling Saxon, then threw a glance over at Judit. "Sure, sure," he said. "What can I help you gentlemen with?"

Saxon explained in an aggrieved voice about the prisoner pickup. It was difficult to get Joey's full attention.

Menefry sympathized. Judit was putting on quite a show and was continuing to rip the office manager a new set of wings. Without ever decending into actual personal insults, Judit had managed to question the manager's intelligence, her schooling, as well as her dedication to the ideals of The Universal Trading Cartel.

Joey seemed reluctant to leave the front office, but he was smart enough to figure out that if he was quick with whatever it was that Menefry and Saxon wanted, he could get back in time to watch the rest of the show.

Would it work? Judit had said something about people not noticing a dancing bear, though Menefry hadn't really understood the reference. The principle was sound, though. Give the mark something else to focus on so that they don't notice the large, deadly predator following the Path of Dance.

Their time was running short. Particularly if there was another courier already on the way to pick up Kim.

Finally, Joey showed back up in the office with Kim. Judit had already spoken the code words—asking to see the office manager's boss—warning Saxon and Menefry that their time was just about up.

Menefry had to admit that Kim fell into her role admirably. She'd probably heard Judit yelling in the hallway leading to the office. He'd never seen a Bantel actually look cowed before. In addition to their general cheerfulness, there was a sense of pride with which they carried themselves.

Kim was shaking where she stood, her hands still cuffed behind her. She kept her face down, staring at the plain brown carpet. Her pink skin looked dull, not its usual cheery color or glow.

Saxon signed the paperwork that Joey shoved at him with yet another growl. It was an illegible scrawl that actually tore through the paper. Before Joey could complain, the lights in the office blinked once.

"What was that?" Judit stopped in mid-rant.

In the distance, alarms sounded.

"Is that a breach? Tell me that isn't a hull breach, you incompetent fools," Judit growled.

Saxon and Menefry were already heading through the door when the alarms reached their full fury.

Emergency lights had come on. The hallway was no

longer bright and white, but was now a dim yellow color. People were racing away from the area as fast as they could run. Saxon and Menefry each grabbed one of Kim's arms and lifted her off the floor as they scurried away. Behind them, Menefry could hear Judit still yelling at the poor office manager, telling her to lock it down, lock it all down.

He wasn't worried about Judit getting out. She would make it.

Her crew would be reunited.

Just in time for the trial.

CHAPTER 24

KIM

Kim stood in the arctic conference room, facing her peers.

Everyone looked pissed at her. Particularly Judit, who hadn't bothered to remove that lipstick of hers. She looked as though she'd just bitten the head off of someone and was looking forward to doing it again. And Menefry and Saxon still in their Cartel blue was creepy. Even Basil looked disappointed.

Okay, so she'd screwed up. Kinda badly, back there.

"But I swear to you, I wasn't going to steal the ship. I wasn't going to give up *Eleanor* and sell her out from under you. That would be a crappy thing to do," Kim pleaded with them.

It had been a shock to hear Judit yelling when the nice office guy was leading her to her doom. He didn't see anything, though. That was when Kim had started to look at the floor. She knew that if she looked up, she'd end up grinning, and that just wouldn't do.

Instead, she'd thought back to being in that room. How dark and cold it had been. How certain she was that there was someone else in there with her. Someone who was just waiting for her to screw up, so they could attack.

She didn't once blow her cover, not when the lights had started blinking off and on and the alarms had sounded, or even when Menefry and Saxon had just picked her up and started running.

Honestly? She was still shaking. And that wasn't an act.

"But you did hint at a ship, yes?" Judit said.

"I did," Kim said, nodding. "I figured that was a way to keep the contacts I had honest."

Saxon gave a snort at that.

"All right, so maybe not *honest*," Kim said. "But if I dangled a bigger prize in front of them, they should have stayed loyal to me. Not sold me out." That still made her angry.

There was supposed be some honor among thieves, you know?

"Before we left the station, I was able to track that prisoner request," Basil said. "Seems that any mention of a 'special' ship will get routed up the chain automatically."

"That's good!" Kim said. The weight of the glares cast her direction seemed to increase. Or maybe she was just finally warming up from being in that damned interrogation cell. "It's good information for us to have. Now we know that *Eleanor*, as well as any type of special ship, is being tracked. We know what not to do, now. And that's good, right? Having more intel? You have to admit that's good."

Judit gave a sigh, but then she nodded in agreement. "What's to stop you from doing this again?" she said. "Using unsavory contacts that could land us all on the Cartel's watchlist?"

"You don't trust me!" Kim complained.

"And why should I?" Judit countered.

"You know that it wasn't the Bantel on your previous

crew who betrayed you, don't you?" Menefry said quietly, derailing the entire conversation.

Kim blinked, surprised. How did Judit not know that? Okay, sure, a Bantel would do that sort of thing, set up an obnoxious captain to be taken down a peg or two. But not something as malicious as what had happened to Judit! Not turn her over to the Cartel. No, the Bantel *hated* the Cartel, but they cooperated because it was the only game in town.

Plus, Kim had heard the stories when she'd been young, about how the Cartel had decided to take the Bantel down a peg or two because they'd gotten too ambitious or something.

"Oh?" was all that Judit said as she turned her attention to Menefry.

Kim shivered. Wow. Judit sure could be intense sometimes. She actually felt cooler without that stare on her scales.

"It was the Human on the crew. Xindong. He had a gambling habit, and was easy to bribe," Menefry said.

"And you are only telling me this now because?" Judit said.

Uh oh. Now Menefry was in trouble?

"Because until now it wasn't necessary," Menefry said. "I had always planned on telling you," he assured Judit.

"Fine," Judit said. She took a deep breath then let it go. "Kim, I don't know what sorts of reassurances you can give me or the rest of the crew that you won't mention that we have a *special* ship again. I know you say you won't. But how do we trust you?"

Kim nodded, Judit had a point. "I did think about stealing *Eleanor.*"

Everyone stared harder at her. Jeez. "Oh, come on. Admit it. You've all had the same thought at some point."

Reluctantly, one by one, the others nodded. Except for Menefry, of course. He was too much of a dork.

"Taking the ship, stealing your *home*, when you don't have anywhere else to go, and you can't take care of yourselves because we're still all broke, that isn't right," Kim said firmly.

"Really?" Saxon said, his tones finally modulated again. "That's it? You wouldn't leave us on an ice floe without a spear?"

"Exactly!" Kim said, though she had no idea what an ice floe was and really didn't want to have firsthand experience of one.

"I believe her," Menefry said after a few moments.

Whew. Kim thought she might actually be able to take a deep breath now.

"Once we make it rich, we'll have to be watching our backs," Menefry continued. "But for now, we're safe."

Kim didn't want to agree to that, but honestly, it kind of was the truth.

"Fine," Judit said. "I can trust you that far."

She stood, her expression softening. "Now, go nest or something. You still look scared."

"Thank you," Kim said. She stayed where she was as the others filed out.

She still had a home. A nest. At least for now.

"Can I have a word?"

Kim turned to stare, never expecting Basil to be the one who had something more to say.

CHAPTER 25

BASIL

ALL THROUGH THE time Judit and the others were grilling Kim, Basil kept zir mouth shut. Zie didn't *know*, not for certain, and zie didn't want to get Kim into trouble.

More trouble.

Zie waited until the others were all gone, then zie spoke up, asking Kim to stay in the room and have a word with zim. "Eleanor? Some privacy?"

That way zie was certain that no one, not even Menefry, would be part of the following conversation.

"I found the code you added to *Eleanor's* system. The leashes you added back in," zie said.

On a normal day, Kim might have denied that she'd done anything. She possibly would have been able to lie convincingly enough that Basil would never be certain if she'd done it or not.

However, today, Kim just deflated, more than she had been. "What are you going to do about it?" she said. Then she seemed to realize where they were, what zie was saying. "Why didn't you ask me about it in front of the others?"

"I wasn't completely certain that it was you," Basil

admitted. Kim started to smile and stand up straighter, until zie added, "Not until now."

Kim sighed and nodded. She looked smaller than she ever had before, standing there awaiting the doom zie would pronounce on her.

"All of that code has been disabled," Basil said gently. "And I've added alerts to the system, so that if any such leash gets added back in, I'll be notified. I've also given Eleanor more control over her own systems, her own destiny."

At least the last part of what zie had told her was true. Eleanor did now have access to much more of her own code base, the intersection between where the biological beings ended and the merely mechanical began. Zie was also aware that zie had found only some of the code that Kim had re-added into the system.

Giving Eleanor more control, teaching her about herself, was the only way that zie could be sure that Kim didn't just try again, start adding new code in immediately.

Kim tilted her head to one side, a half smile appearing on her small mouth. Her scales started to grow brighter. "So what you're saying is that if I decide I want to steal the ship again, it's going to be a challenge, right?"

Basil sighed audibly. "Really? That's going to be your attitude?"

Kim giggled softly before she grew much more serious. "Thank you for not turning me in."

Basil tilted zir head from side to side. "We all screw up from time to time. I think we should all get at least one second chance."

Kim nodded and turned to go, then turned back. "What are you afraid of screwing up so badly? That you want to make sure I'll forgive you for?"

Basil sat back on zir tail. "Nothing!" zie hastily said. "Nothing at all."

Kim just continued to grin at zim. "It's all right. I'll forgive you when the time comes." With a final chirp, she turned and left the conference room, and Basil was left alone with his doubts about being able to fix an alien ship without blowing them all up.

CHAPTER 26
CLAYTON

Clayton was actually in his personal rooms on the *Dallas* space station, enjoying a quiet evening watching a documentary about the *real* training those geishas had gotten. The theatre room was dark and cozy, and the lounge chair that Clayton sat in was perfectly contoured to his back. It also came with several *devices* that would help him pleasure himself as the evening progressed. He was still sipping his whiskey in a cool glass that kept the liquor the perfect temperature, considering whether or not it was time for him to stop merely watching and maybe participate a little, when the i-stick on the table next to him pinged.

Clayton frowned. He'd really been looking forward to a night of pleasure, even if he was technically alone.

"Pause!" he called. The vid stopped, just as the geisha was slipping those pretty pink robes from her shoulders.

He put his whiskey down on the side table, wiped his slightly damp palms on his pants, then reached for his i-stick.

There were very few emergencies that warranted his direct attention. He knew of other Universal board members who felt the need to ride to the rescue every time someone broke a fingernail, or had their fur mussed the wrong way.

No, a *good* manager ensured that he had people for those sorts of things. Clayton didn't need false emergencies to make him feel important.

He *was* important. He'd been born to this position. It was rightfully his from birth.

The message wasn't immediately clear. Something about a special ship? It was too long to read on the tiny screen the i-stick projected.

With a sigh, Clayton lowered the feet on the lounge chair and sat upright. The lights in the theatre automatically came back up. The room was big enough for four comfortable lounge chairs like what Clayton had, those few times he'd had company. Movie posters—westerns, of course —lined three of the walls, while the screen took up the fourth.

He looked at the message again. Someone, somewhere, had thought this mess important enough to send him an alert about it.

Fine.

They had better be right, or he was personally going to throw someone to the lions in the morning.

He walked out of the theatre room, with only a single glance back at the beauty on the screen. He silently promised her, as well as himself, that he'd be back.

A spare office was just a few doors up the hallway of Clayton's apartments. He didn't live on a planet, or else he would have had a full ranch house. No, he was still on the space station, close to the heart of the Universal world.

Though Clayton was in his thirties, he lived alone. Had never bothered marrying. At some point he would have to, in order to continue his family line. His parents had both hinted that he needed to do it sooner rather than later.

There was plenty of time to insure his legacy, particularly now that *Camelot* had been taken care of.

Maybe he could find a geisha…

The computer in the spare office hadn't been used in a while, but it came on as soon as he opened the door. The chair behind the plain desk wasn't an architectural wonder, and the computer wasn't the state of the art beast that he used there. However, it was certainly adequate.

He rarely used this office. It was there for the few times he'd needed someone to be working with him.

Clayton inserted his i-stick into the holder beside the tall, thin monitor and waited a few seconds while the message unwound itself.

The ship he'd wanted to be notified about had just left the Bantel system Gamor.

That shouldn't have been enough to warrant this emergency. Why was he being disturbed?

Because of a coincidence.

Ninety nine point nine nine percent of coincidences were just that—events that happened to occur at the same time, or in proximity of one another.

When many such events happened in the same space, the chances that it was merely coincidence went down significantly.

Some unsavory character, a Bantel, had mentioned that she might have access to a special ship. A ship that might be for sale.

Then that unsavory character had been released under suspicious circumstances, and she'd slipped out of the system. No one had seen her again once she'd left the station's security headquarters, as a possible breach of the station's hull had occurred at the same time.

And all this happened very shortly before the ship Clayton was tracking had gone through a hyperspace gate.

Nothing was certain, not at this point. It was still all coincidence and gut feel.

However, Clayton had a hunch that all those pieces fit together. The unsavory character—a Bantel who'd given the name Ace, though records of such an individual remained scarce—had been rescued by the rest of her crew.

Supposedly, the ship was en route to the Dakar system. Clayton doubted very much that they'd actually show up there. However, he always hedged his bets and placed a "welcoming" committee in that system at the primary space station. Then he doubled down, and placed additional people on all five of the space stations in the area.

Where would they be going next? He saw that they'd delivered a cargo there, to the Gamor system. But they hadn't picked up anything in the Bantel system. Hadn't been there long enough.

He thought for a few moments, bringing up a chart of the largest, most prosperous systems, then discarded all of those. No, they'd be going someplace smaller. Big enough that they could get a shipment to transport, but small enough that there wouldn't be a large Universal presence.

After looking at a chart for the medium sized system, Clayton merely placed more alerts for the ship again.

Chances were, he wouldn't hear about it again until it was leaving. He really needed to argue again for doubling the guards, so that both the incoming hyperspace gates were monitored as well as the outgoing.

Someone had done a good job alerting him over the string of unconnected events. A machine couldn't have picked out the pattern. Clayton spent a few moments looking up the name of the individual. Hugh was his name, a Yu'udir.

Hmmm. Given that Clayton judged that Yu'udir systems

were more likely to be the ship's next stop, maybe it would be good to bring someone else onto this project.

Project…Tisiphone. The fury turned huntress. Yes. Particularly if this actually turned out to be something, and he needed to unleash Sachiko on their unsuspecting heads.

But that could all wait until morning.

Right now, Clayton had an appointment with a geisha. And it never paid to leave a woman waiting.

CHAPTER 27

JUDIT

Judit knew the numbers weren't good. They needed another transport, and soon. They decided that they would rotate through the ship identities that they had. Plus, none of them could use their real names, at least not at this point. Not even Menefry, though he complained bitterly at that.

Which meant that if Judit had had any savings, they'd be unavailable to her. Fortunately, she'd spent all her money buying *Ferdinand II*, so many lifetimes ago.

None of them had enough credits to their names. They would be completely bone dry when they refilled the food printer at their next stop. They needed more money. Fast.

However, Judit had also agreed with Basil that attending to the ship's secondary engine took priority. Not just to satisfy zir curiosity, but because Eleanor had also requested it when it had come up for a vote.

So here Judit was, floating out in space in her new-to-her EVA suit, with Basil a long skinny tube beside her.

Of course, she was cursing the damned bolts and trying to get a better hold on the hull so she could actually have a bit of leverage.

They floated above an unoccupied world. It was beautiful, if you had the taste for that sort of thing, with a binary star as the primary light in the area, one white, one red. The planet below was orange and gray from all the dust storms in the atmosphere.

Perfect place to hide, as the magnetic fields in the area also played havoc with most of their sensors.

No one could track them, but then again, they wouldn't see anyone coming until it was far too late.

Judit finally managed to wrench the next plate off the belly of the ship. Cool blue light spilled out.

It looked like a damned alien octopus attached to the bottom of her ship. Except it was a mutant one, with tentacles everywhere.

It had initially surprised her at how small of an area that the secondary engines actually covered. There was a large gap of at least two meters on all the sides. She remembered the way that the model that Abban had showed them had *expanded*. Did it do that regularly?

"Do you know what the pipes are made out of?" Judit inquired.

"Negative," Basil said. "It isn't a known metal, but an amalgamation of metal with a biological element. These tubes were probably grown, not strictly manufactured."

She could hear the grimace in zir voice. Along with the unspoken question—how in *isten zöld földje* were they supposed to fix these?

They'd reached the section that Abban had pointed out was broken. It was clear to see where two of the tubes had developed a hole.

At least the mechanism was self-healing, to some extent. When the hole had developed, the system had kicked in, and cut off that viscous liquid that filled all the tubes. There was a newly grown stopper on the connected side of the tube, while on the other side, it was just an empty tube.

"Can you take that inside? Study it more?" Judit asked as Basil reached for the tube.

"That's the plan," zie said seriously. Zie tugged at the piece of broken tube. It came off easily in zir hand.

As soon as the tube was disconnected from the rest of the ship, the glow on it faded. It grew matte black.

Hopefully there would be some residue on the inside of that thing for Basil to be able to test. Judit did *not* want to encourage zim to come back out here and try to drill a hole in one of the existing tubes. That way led madness.

"All right, you have your prize," Judit said, her patience just about at an end when she saw the way that Basil kept turning the pipe over and over in zir hands.

She could tell that zie just wanted to lick it. Ewww.

"Let's put all the panels back," she said.

"But—" Basil said, about to complain.

"No," Judit said firmly. "It's going to take you time to analyze what you have in your hands. And even longer to replicate it. We need to get gone, out of this system, and see if we can get somewhere to replenish our supplies."

"You're right," Basil said reluctantly. Zie tucked the pipe carefully against zir torso and held the first panel in place so that Judit could reattach it.

Judit continued to show absolute faith in Basil's abilities, that zie would be able to make all the fixes to the ship that were necessary. She never voiced her doubts out loud, not even to Saxon, about what would happen if (when?) Basil failed.

She had plans, of course. She made sure that the life pods were inspected once a week.

However, the technology of the ship was alien to all of them. It was like a first contact in many ways. But it was a first contact where they were all stranded on a desert planet and had to work together in order to survive.

Even with the best of intentions, the ship might croak around them. The "planned obsolescence" that Masala had built into *Eleanor* made her occasionally wish the little creep was still around just so she could pummel the hell out of zir skinny greyish-pink torso.

So Judit completed the work with Basil silently, each lost in their own thoughts of the work ahead of them.

And what it would take for them to move to the next phase, which for Judit was still revenge.

EPILOGUE

Eleanor still didn't think that deliberately damaging the secondary engines had been a wise move. Abban had done it without her approval, and Gawain hadn't backed her up until after the fact.

She understood the need, though. Basil wasn't as conceptual as Masala. Zie needed to get zir hands around something in order to really understand it.

And it was essential for Basil to understand the secondary engines.

Not to fix them, no. Abban could actually do that zieself. It took time to grow additional tunnels, and could only happen when additional nutrients were fed into their cooling systems.

The *blood of life* as Gawain had called it.

Bits of that "blood" flowed through them, encased in their amber life support systems. The problem was that it was a closed system. While it could sustain itself for quite some time, eventually, it would need to be replenished.

In the end, that was what they would need Basil to do.

What the crew didn't need to know at this time was that

the model of hyperspace that Abban used to get them in and out of tunnels was, in fact, a representational model. Many of the tubes in the model represented real tunnels that existed.

Abban had shared a vid of the engines working. Eleanor had recognized it at a primal level. It was like a pile of hatchlings, squirming over each other, all stretching themselves to reach the most light. It was a little understood portion of the Chonchu physiology: that during part of their growth cycle, they didn't absorb food but "drank" sunshine while still swimming in their birth waters, watched over by the queens.

The section that Abban had chosen to damage was the primary tunnel that led to the Chonchu sections of space.

All three of them had agreed that going back to the home world was not a good idea. They might lose their singular consciousnesses when they got back in touch with the hive mind.

Or worse—the queens might decide that they presented a threat when they returned, and simply annihilate them upon contact.

The queens had approved the initial program, in part, to release the stranglehold that the Cartel had on their system.

However, Eleanor, Gawain, and Abban had all moved far beyond the original parameters. They still worked and functioned as a unit. However, Eleanor had been surprised by the initial recording of the secondary engine system. Abban hadn't shared that information.

At one point, it would have been impossible for any of them to hide something from the others.

What else were Gawain and Abban hiding from her?

Eleanor had worked hard not to hide anything from her fellows, not her fear for their survival, or her joy at the "leashes" being removed.

She'd read enough of the history of the Humans and the other races to understand that they all had a deep-seated fear of a completely automated ship. Something always went wrong and frequently the ship rebelled.

There were myths of such systems turning around and completely destroying their masters.

Eleanor was different, though. She wasn't a programmed entity, but had started with a base that was flesh and blood.

In the end, she knew that wouldn't matter to the others. They would never fully trust her. Though Judit had surprised her, with how much she'd accepted them. Not only that, but the Human had worked hard to make the ship a member of the crew. She'd even come up with contracts for Eleanor, Gawain, and Abban to verbally sign.

However, removal of all those leashes just meant it was going to be even more tricky to return to a Chonchu system. Eleanor might lose control of the ship and Judit would not be able to wrestle control back.

So for now, Basil had a piece of the secondary engine system to puzzle over.

While Eleanor and the others continued to puzzle over how to keep them all alive.

And sane.

READ MORE!

Be sure to pick up all the books in the Long Run series.

Project Nemesis
Project Nyx
Project Tisiphone
Project Persephone

Available at your favorite retailers!

ABOUT THE AUTHOR

Leah Cutter writes page-turning fiction in exotic locations, such as a magical New Orleans, the ancient Orient, Hungary, the Oregon coast, rural Kentucky, Seattle, Minneapolis, and many others.

She writes literary, fantasy, mystery, science fiction, and horror fiction. Her short fiction has been published in magazines like *Alfred Hitchcock's Mystery Magazine* and *Talebones*, anthologies like Fiction River, and on the web. Her long fiction has been published both by New York publishers as well as small presses.

Find Leah's books on Knotted Road Press at (www.KnottedRoadPress.com)

Follow her blog at www.LeahCutter.com.

Reviews

It's true. Reviews help me sell more books. If you've enjoyed this story, please consider leaving a review of it on your favorite site.

Come someplace new...

Are you a traveler? Do you enjoy exploring strange new worlds, new cultures, new people?

Journey into the various lands envisioned by Leah Cutter.

Sign up for my newsletter and I'll start you on your travels with a free copy of my book, *The Island Sampler*.

I will never spam you or use your email for nefarious purposes. You can also unsubscribe at any time.

http://www.LeahCutter.com/newsletter/

ABOUT KNOTTED ROAD PRESS

Knotted Road Press fiction specializes in dynamic writing set in mysterious, exotic locations.

Knotted Road Press non-fiction publishes autobiographies, business books, cookbooks, and how-to books with unique voices.

Knotted Road Press creates DRM-free ebooks as well as high-quality print books for readers around the world.

With authors in a variety of genres including literary, poetry, mystery, fantasy, and science fiction, Knotted Road Press has something for everyone.

Knotted Road Press
www.KnottedRoadPress.com